Amos Tutuola was born in Abeokuta, Nigeria, in 1920. The son of a cocoa farmer, he attended several schools before training as a blacksmith. He later worked as a civil servant. His first novel, *The Palm-Wine Drinkard*, was published in 1952 and brought him international recognition. From 1956 until retirement, he worked for the Nigerian Broadcasting Company while continuing to write. His last book, *The Village Witch Doctor and Other Stories*, was published in 1990. He died in Ibadan in 1997.

T0322944

Simbi and the Satyr of the Dark Jungle

AMOS TUTUOLA

FABER & FABER

This edition first published in 2015
by Faber & Faber Ltd
The Bindery, 51 Hatton Garden,
London ECIN 8HN

Typeset by Faber & Faber Ltd
Printed in England by CPI Group (UK) Ltd, Croydon, CRO 4YY

A CIP record for this book is available from the British Library

ISBN 978-0-571-32072-1

The Life of Simbi, the most beautiful girl in the Village

Simbi was the daughter of a wealthy woman, and she was an only issue of her mother.

She was not working at all, except to eat and after that to bathe and then to wear several kinds of the costliest garments. Although she was a wonderful singer whose beautiful voice could wake deads and she was only the most beautiful girl in the village.

Having eaten the nice food, bathed and dressed in the morning, the next thing that which she was doing was to be singing about in the village.

Simbi was the most merry making girl in the village and in respect of that almost the whole people of her village liked to see her every time. Especially for her singing and amusing sayings, and she was pleased with her mother's wealths.

Simbi had two friends named Rali and Sala. Both were accompanying her to wherever she was going to sing. They could not be happy without seeing each other in a moment.

One morning, Simbi went to visit these her two friends.

But she was greatly terrified when she did not meet both at home, because such a thing had never happened between them before. And she was nearly to faint when she heard the information from the reliable source that Rali and Sala were kidnapped from the path by an unknown man. Then she came back to her mother's house with grief.

For several days, Simbi was unable to eat, she did not drink water and did not sing as well and did not happy, except to see her two friends.

Of course, a few weeks after, the love of her friends was fading gradually from her heart, and then she started to eat a little food, but she stopped singing entirely.

A few months after that her friends had been kidnapped or had left the village, Simbi became tired of her mother's wealths and became entirely tired to be in happiness, etc. that which her mother's wealths were giving to her.

"I am now entirely fed up with my mother's wealths. I can no longer bear to remain in the happiness, etc., giving me by my mother's wealths. And merriments are now too much for me than what I can bear longer than this time. But the only things that I prefer most to know and experience their difficulties now are the 'Poverty' and the 'Punishment'." It was like that Simbi thought within herself, because the had never experienced neither the difficulties of the poverty nor had experienced the difficulties of the punishment since when she was born.

CHAPTER ONE

Mother! I like to know the Poverties and Punishments

One afternoon, Simbi's mother and with her friend who came to her house, were discussing on a matter which concerned the poverty and punishment. And in the discussions they were mentioning the words—"Poverty" and "Punishment" often and often. But Simbi who stood by them did not understand the meanings of the two words. A few minutes after, her mother's friend went back to her house having finished their discussions.

But as Simbi had kept the two words in mind once she had heard them mentioned, she called her mother to a room and with great respect she asked "Please my mother I shall be very happy if you will allow me to go abroad from where I will experience the difficulties of the 'Poverty' and of the 'Punishment'."

"Will you shut up your mouth, Simbi, for asking me of what the whole people are praying of every minute not to know and experience until they shall die!" her mother warned her seriously and then drove her out of the room at once.

Throughout that day, Simbi was not happy at all and she

did not take any food, because her intention was just to know the "Poverty" and "Punishment" at all costs. And a few days after, she asked the same question from her mother. But she drove her out of the room as the first time.

When Simbi was quite sure that her mother had refused to approve her request, she went to an old man, she asked for the meanings of the "Poverty" and of the "Punishment".

"Hah! Simbi, don't try to know the meanings of the 'Poverty' and 'Punishment'. The 'Poverty' and 'Punishment' are far beyond of what a young girl like you shall try to know or to experience. Go back to your wealthy mother! She is wealthy enough in everything and she can satisfy you in all of your needs. Simbi, go back to your wealthy mother!" with astonishment the old man warned Simbi loudly.

"Never mind about my mother's wealths, old Pa, but I like to be wealthy in 'Poverty' and in 'Punishment' as well as my mother is wealthy in money, etc.!"

"Simbi, don't try to know the 'Poverty' and the 'Punishment' and that is the only useful advice which I can give you," the old man added strongly.

"Old Pa! I say I like to know the 'Poverty' and the 'Punishment'," Simbi repeated it painfully to the old man. And when the old man's advice as well as her mother's was against her wish, she came back to the house. But she still kept the matter in mind.

Now, Simbi was always thinking seriously of the way she could know the two words and to experience their difficulties. And again she was not happy at all in respect

of her two friends, Rali and Sala, who had been kidnapped
by an unknown man.

Having thought about these two words for a few weeks
without sleeping at night, she remembered to go to the
soothsayer who could solve the words to her.

Then early in the morning, she stole one penny out of
her mother's money. She said to the penny, "What are
the meanings of the 'poverty' and the 'punishment' and
how to experience their difficulties?"

Having said like that to the penny, she threw it into
her pocket and then kept going to the soothsayer's house.
When she reached there, she met him sat attentively
before the tray of his Ifa, the god of oracle, and the tray
contained sixteen cowries as well.

"Good morning, the soothsayer!" she saluted him.
"Hallo! good morning to you, girl, and the Ifa answers
you as well," he delivered the Ifa's message to her. Because Ifa was answering the salutation as well.

Having saluted him, she told him that she came to him
just to find out some secret matter, she did not tell him
frankly of what she came there for, and the soothsayer
himself did not want any explanation before what she
came for had been solved.

At the same time, he re-arranged the sixteen cowries in
good order, for they had scattered all over the wooden
tray in which they were always. And it were these sixteen
cowries were going to explain to the soothsayer in the
code words of what Simbi wanted to know, and after he
had studied the code words, then he would explain it to
Simbi in plain words.

11

Then Simbi put the penny on the cowries. Having cast the cowries on the tray several times and having studied the code words which the cowries said, then he explained to her as follows:

"You see, Simbi, the Ifa, the god of oracle, says that at all costs you shall know what your intention likes to know and you shall experience its difficulties even farther than as you are expecting it to be.

"But before it can be so, you ought to make two kinds of sacrifices. Firstly, you will sacrifice one cock to your head. The cock must be of three years of age. And to sacrifice the cock to your head means to safe your life throughout your journey and to help you to return to your mother. Because you will travel for many years and it is in your travel you will know and experience of what you ask now from the Ifa, the god of oracle.

"And secondly, after you have sacrificed the cock to your head, you will buy one dog, one bottle of palm oil, plenty of bitter colas and the cola nuts, one broken pot and one pigeon. You will kill the dog and after you have cut it into two parts, you will put them inside the broken pot. Then you will behead the pigeon and put it inside the pot as well.

"Having done all that, you will split those cola nuts and put them together with the bitter colas inside the pot. And then you will pour the palm oil on top of all the preparations.

"After that, you will keep the sacrifice in a safe place where it will remain till five o'clock in the morning when you will carry it by head to the junction of three paths and you will put it down there, but you must not look at your back when you are carrying it along to the junction.

"After you have put it down, you will kneel down before it (sacrifice), then you will start to pray for what your intention likes to know and experience.

"And it will be a great surprise to you that before you shall say the prayer to the end one man will come unexpectedly from your back, believe that it is the sacrifice brings the man. At the same time he will hold your both arms and without hesitation he will be dragging you mercilessly along one of that paths to a foreign town in which he will sell you as a slave, and you must believe that that is the path of death.

"And it is from that junction you will start to know and experience of what your intention likes to know, etc.," thus the soothsayer explained to Simbi.

"Good! you are a well qualified soothsayer in deed, for you have solved what I asked from the Ifa." After these explanations Simbi lay down flatly and thanked the soothsayer greatly, and then she came back to her mother's house with gladness.

Alas! Simbi did not believe that a young girl like herself must not attempt to force herself to know of what her parents had warned her for, not to attempt to know.

The very day that the soothsayer had explained to Simbi the right kinds of sacrifices which she would make, and her mother being wealthy, therefore she had the privilege, she stole a large sum of money from her mother's money without any suspicion. With the money she bought the dog, pigeon, the broken pot and the rest things.

In the evening, she sacrificed the cock to her head, so that she might be able to return safely to her mother having vanished for several years, thus the soothsayer had explained to her.

And in the night she killed the dog, she cut it to two parts, and after, she beheaded the pigeon, she put it together with the dog inside the broken pot. Then she put the cola nuts, etc. inside the same pot, after, she poured the palm oil on top of all the preparations, and then she kept this sacrifice in a safe corner of the room, so that her mother might not see it.

By five o'clock in the morning, she woke by the cocks which were crowing loudly every where in the village. She got up from the mat, and she went to the corner where she had put the sacrifice, and she put it on the head.

After that, she opened the door, she got to the outside and then shut the door back so cautiously that her mother together with the rest family did not wake at all from sleep. And from there she carried the sacrifice without looking at her back, to the junction of three paths, and she put it down there. The junction was about two miles from the village.

CHAPTER TWO

Simbi and Dogo on the
Path of Death

After Simbi had put down the sacrifice, she knelt down before it, and as she was praying "I make this sacrifice and bring it here, just to help me to know the 'Poverty' and the 'Punishment' and to experience their difficulties, and also . . ."

A very tall man came from her back and at the same time he held her arms and head backward. He drew the head toward himself so violently that Simbi stood up suddenly without her wish.

The name of this terrible man was Dogo. Dogo was an expert kidnapper of children and he was a native of a town called the "Sinners' town", the town in which only sinners and worshippers of gods were living. Dogo had no other work more than to be travelling on every path and kidnapping another people's children and then selling them as slaves for the foreigners. But only this Path of Death led to his town and the town was too far and too fearful for other people to go there, hence it was among some towns which were the last to the end of the world, perhaps.

15

Simbi and Dogo on the Path of Death

And it was from this junction Simbi started to receive the punishment, according to what her soothsayer had told her.

At the same moment, Dogo was pushing Simbi along one of that three paths, and that was the Path of Death. At the first instance she tried to snatch herself back from Dogo and then return to her village. But he did not give her the chance. Instead, he was just slapping both her ears and dragging her along. And she had lost all her senses within a few minutes.

"Who are you pushing me along mercilessly like this?" Simbi asked with the trembling voice when she became conscious.

"Dogo, the kidnapper, please," he replied sharply. "To where are you pushing me now?" she asked painfully.

"I am pushing you to another town in which I shall sell you," he replied simply.

But when Simbi heard so, she stopped firmly on both feet at the centre of the path.

"I want to go back to my mother now," she told Dogo horribly.

"By the way what is your name?" Dogo asked wildly.

"My name? My name is Simbi," she sneezed and then replied softly.

"Simbi?" he repeated the name. Simbi hesitated for a few seconds and then said "Yes!" disrespectfully.

"Huh o! is that so? all right, keep going, and that is the name with which your buyer will be calling you or if you are unlucky, he shall give you a different name which is suitable for a slave!"

"Keeping going to where, Mr. Dogo?" Simbi asked without being feared of any number of the heavy slaps that he might give her.

"To where I am going to sell you now," he explained simply. "Sell me? No! you cannot do that," she wondered.

Having said like that and still she insisted to keep going. Then Dogo struck both her eyes with his thick palm. And without mercy he pushed her so heavily that she dashed to a tree nearby, and at the same moment she fell flatly on the path as if she had already dead.

After a few minutes that she became conscious, she told Dogo loudly "Don't be stupid, man! Let me go back to my mother!"

"To go back to your mother?" Dogo responded and laughed greatly. "Oh yes! don't you know that my mother is the most wealthy woman in my village?" she explained boldly, perhaps Dogo would release her to go back.

"Of course, your mother may be a millionaire, that does not concern me in any way. But I am taking you to where I am going to sell you and then to spend the money that I sell you for all my needs, hence am not entitled to your mother's wealths," he replied to simply as if Simbi was a fowl that he was going to sell.

"Don't you know that it is entirely wrong and shameful to sell the daughter of a wealthy woman like me, and furthermore my mother has no other issue except I alone?"

"Of course, I don't know! and I don't want to know

whether you are the daughter of a wealthy woman, just keep going to where I am going to sell you," he replied so horribly that Simbi thought she had already dead.

"But if you take me back to my mother now and sell me back to her, I am quite sure that she will pay you even a larger amount of money than a foreigner who will buy me can pay for you." she suggested calmly.

"Of course, that is a useful advice which you are quite right to give, and that is useful only for you, but it is entirely useless to me. For it will cause a serious trouble to me if I take you back to your mother, hence it is impossible for a mother to see the captor of her daughter without arresting him for the police," Dogo explained and he rejected her advice.

When Simbi believed that everything had come to the climax, she confessed painfully, "If that is so, Dogo, I shall confess to you now that the reason why you met me at the junction and then caught me, was that I had wanted to know the 'Poverty' and the 'Punishment' and to experience also their difficulties. But I have now declined from my wish in respect of the severe punishments which you are giving me continuously since when you have caught me about one hour ago.

"And it is this day, I believe that it is entirely bad for a young girl like me to determine to know the 'Poverty' and the 'Punishment'. Hence those who are now in poverty and punishment are praying every minute to free from them. But I admit that I have made a great mistake.

18

Simbi and Dogo on the Path of Death

"Although, my wealthy mother and with several old people of my village, had already warned me seriously for not attempting to know them (Poverty and Punishment), but I did not pay heed to their warning, my ears rejected the warning as a 'nonsense'.

"I beg you, Dogo, my captor, to have mercy on me and set me free and let me go back now to my mother, otherwise she will be puzzled probably to death in a few days' time, if she does not see me to return home."

"Is that so, Simbi? You are lucky then as I kidnapped you this very day that you brought the sacrifice to the junction, which was to help you to know the 'Poverty' etc. And I congratulate you highly that you are a brave girl indeed who determines not to face the freedom but the difficulties of the 'Poverty' and of the 'Punishment' etc.

"Hear me now, Simbi, it is very disgraceful for a brave girl like you to decline from her wish without seeing the end of what she has determined to know.

"I am quite sure, in a few days' time you shall know the 'Poverty' and the 'Punishment', even you shall see them personally. And you shall experience their difficulties even farther than as you are expecting them to be. Because the difficulties of the 'Poverty' etc. are almost without the end.

"Now, I call your attention back to the matter of setting you free and to have also mercy on you. I can confess to you now, Simbi, that the more I, Dogo, kidnap a boy or girl there is no anything like mercy for him or her at all, and I have never released any of my captives in my life. But I shall sell him or her at all costs whomever he or she may be, and that is my policy from the beginning. Therefore, I am very sorry to tell you now that I shall not depart from this rule, simply because your wealthy mother has no another issue except you alone!

"Hah! Simbi, you want to know and experience the 'Poverty' and the 'Punishment'? And I assure you now that you shall know them to the very end. And to add more to my explanations. You are now on the Path of Death. Of course, I cannot blame you, because 'the dog which will lose will not answer the call and will not pay heed to the call of its keeper'.

"Therefore, Simbi, there is no need for a person who has already fallen into the water to escape for the cold and you are the very person who has fallen into the water," Dogo explained distinctly.

But Simbi was greatly terrified when she heard that it was on the Path of Death she was. Because she had been hearing several times from her family and from other people that any one who travelled on this path, was going to die.

"Keep going now girl! and the only promise that I can give you is that I am going to sell you in a town which is near this Path of Death!

"The dog which will lose will not pay heed to the call of its master. That means if you have paid heed to your mother's warning you should have not met this punishment," Dogo repeated and then he commanded her to keep going.

And when she refused to keep going, Dogo slapped her

at head so heavily that she started to feel headache at the same time, and he was pushing her along the Path of Death with his own hands.

Having travelled till the evening they came to a town. This town was so far away from Simbi's village that she could not even trace out the right path to her village, even if she had the chance to escape.

CHAPTER THREE

Simbi in the town where nobody sings

Dogo took Simbi to a big shop immediately they entered the town. It was an auctioneer's shop and there was a very wide, flat ground at the front of this shop. It was on that ground the auctioneer used to sell all articles or slaves which or who were to be sold very urgently.

After Dogo had explained to the auctioneer that he wanted him to sell Simbi by urgent, for he wanted the quick money for buying food, then the auctioneer first put Simbi on the weighing scale just to know her exact weight which would enable him to know the real price that he would impose upon her.

Having quite sure of her real weight, he wore several oversized garments for her. Each of the garments was sewn with about twenty yards of cloth.

After that, he put on her head an oversized hat which swallowed her head so that she was terrible to see at that moment. All these dresses made Simbi bigger than her usual size.

After, he put a sofa at the centre of the ground. Simbi sat on it and he compelled her also to swell out every part of her body with pride so that she might be seemed to every intended buyer that she was pleased for selling her. Then a number of the appraisers seated on two benches at a little distance from her. After this arrangement, the touting man of the auctioneer came with a big bell and he stood at the front of her.

Within ten minutes that the touting man was ringing the bell loudly more than one thousand people heard the bell and came there. They surrounded Simbi who was greatly surprised to see herself in this condition.

After a while, the darkness of the night came and she could not be seen clearly from the sofa. Then the auctioneer lighted his big "fitila", he put it nearly to touch her face. Its brown flame shone to all over her body and also to some part of the ground, but there was still darkness at the back of the ground.

When the auctioneer noticed that enough people had gathered there, he stood up and announced loudly with the voice of business, "Yes, give an offer!" Then those appraisers started their business. They were raising the price of Simbi up and up and up together with those intended buyers. And a few minutes later, every one of the buyers was greedily raising up the price so that Simbi might fall in his hand.

Having seen this, the appraisers insisted on twenty thousand cowries for which to sell her. At that stage, it became the matter of bribery. "No bribe, no Simbi!" was the slogan saying of the appraisers and the auctioneer. And it was so those people were pressing her body with hands every time just to make sure how fat she was. And

23

a few minutes later she became unconscious suddenly because she was nearly pressed to death.

Before she became conscious, those people had scattered in the darkness at the back of the ground. Everyone of them was calling the appraisers, the auctioneer, and the touting man up and down and he was bribing them with money. But at last a rich man who was among, bribed the auctioneer with a very considerable amount that he was happily accepted. Of course, when this revealed to the rest intended buyers, they disordered at once and started to fight each other instead to fight the rich man, for they could not distinguish one from another in the darkness.

However, Simbi fell into the hand of the rich man. Then she was escorted by the touting man to the auctioneer, appraisers and the rich man and she stood before them. And on her presence the rich man paid the amount for which he bought her to Dogo. Having seen this, Simbi asked painfully "Do you sell me in the darkness, Dogo?" "Yes," he replied sharply. Because it was just revealed to her at that moment, that she was put on that sofa for sale, though she had been thinking within herself that those people were going to instal her the queen of that town. And it was from that darkness she was taken to the rich man's slave yard.

But to everyone's surprise, it was in this town Dogo had spent such a considerable amount of money for food and gambling before he left for his town.

Immediately Simbi was mercilessly pushed inside the slave yard of the rich man who was then her master. All the wide slave girls rushed to her. She was first welcomed with several blows that which made her to dash to the pillars and wall before she fell on the ground helplessly at the same time.

After a while, she became conscious, then she stood up with both feet which were shaking for the pain of the sudden blows. Having managed and stood up, those slave girls were pushing her again from one to another and from the pillars to the wall. They left her when she was about to die and then they explained to her "We are now pleased to have you in our company. Because a new comer like you must be first served with blows instead with food!"

It was after Simbi was left to beat when she noticed that many of the junior slaves were chained and laid on the ground since about one week. There the rain was scorching and the heat of the sun was beating them. Because they offended "myrmidon" who had the right to punish any of the junior slaves to death, if her offence so deserved to do.

"Yay! no doubt, I shall die in this yard," Simbi feared immediately she had seen those who were chained and laid on the ground.

"Not yet the time you shall die here, just sit down and let me sit down on your head, for I feel to rest for a few hours," the myrmidon said sharply. Willing or not Simbi sat on the ground and the myrmidon sat on her head and then she (myrmidon) was enjoying herself. And Simbi was still in this condition when a junior slave brought half cooked food to her. But in respect of the heavy weight of the myrmidon, she was unable to eat the food. Although she had never eaten anything since when she had been caught from the junction by Dogo.

25

Simbi in the town where nobody sings

When the myrmidon noticed that she did not eat the food but she was simply looking at it, she ordered one of the junior slaves to beat her and she was beaten nearly to death, while she (myrmidon) was on her head.

"Ah! my mother had warned me not to attempt to know the 'Poverty' and the 'Punishment'!" suffering forced Simbi to remember.

"Which means your mother had already warned you? Let us hint you, you have never received any punishment here, but we are still playing with you as if you are a gentlewoman!" several slaves exclaimed. Having heard this again, Simbi sighed and said aloud "I die today!" For she was sweating continuously at that moment for the heavy weight that which was on her head.

They were not singing at all in this town. Even beating of any kind of the drums, laughing, joking, or merry making were entirely banned there. Because if they did one of these things nearly the whole people of the town would die without special reason. Because their gods disliked any kind of the merriment.

In the following morning, Simbi followed the rest slave girls to the farm of their master. They worked from the morning till when the darkness came. Within a few minutes that she started to work with the rest, both her palms were bruised and were so paining her that she could not touch anything with them (palms). Because she had never worked since when she was born, but she was only singing about.

"You are too lazy, Simbi!" the rest slaves were always repeating that after they had punished here severely.

Simbi in the town where nobody sings

One mid-night, when she believed that if she continued to be working along with her colleagues like that, she would die in a few days' time, she thought of what she could be doing that which could satisfy her colleagues. But as she had been an expert singer before she was kidnapped by Dogo, she remembered one of her long songs before the day-break, and she kept it in mind to sing it for them early in the morning. Whereas such a thing as this must not happen in this town, but she did not know about that.

And it was not yet early in the morning when Simbi started to sing the song. She was singing it on and on and on until it woke the rest slave girls, her master and his family and many people of that area.

Her master was running furiously to the yard just to check her to stop singing, immediately he heard her singing. Unfortunately when he entered the yard, he stumbled his right leg against a stub, he fell down suddenly and then he died at the same time. And when all her master's family heard the news they rushed into the yard.

Having seen the rich man, Simbi's master, lay helplessly on the ground, all exclaimed "Yay!—ay! Simbi, you have killed your master!" "Not I at all! I am not the one who killed him!" "You are the one! It was your song killed him!" the family of the rich man insisted loudly.

At the same time, one of the family suggested "It is better to beat Simbi now to death with a cudgel just to revenge from her at once!"

"Oh! don't let us beat her to death. To beat her to death immediate does not severe enough as the kind of a

27

punishment that which her offence deserves. But my own suggestion is to stab her at heart with a pointed knife and leave the knife there till she will suffer to death!" another man suggested.

"No! to stab her to death does not severe enough. But my own suggestion is to make a solid coffin of plank. Then we will put her alive inside the coffin and after that the lid of the coffin will be nailed. Having done that we will carry the coffin to a river and throw it there. Therefore the tide will be carrying the coffin about until Simbi will be suffered to death," another one of the family suggested.

"Very good! we do agree to your suggestion!" the rest family exclaimed.

One hour later, the coffin was brought. They dressed her with three big garments out of her master's garments, they put on her head one of his hats, one long sword which was in the sheath was hung on her left shoulder, they forced her to hold one walking stick with left hand and a shot gun with right hand, all these things belonged to her master.

After that, they put her master's smoking pipe with plenty of tobacco leaves inside his juju-bag, which he would be smoking along the heaven road and in the heaven and they put his shaving knife inside the bag as well, with which he would be shaving his beard, etc. in the heaven. And then cooking pots, plates, etc. oil, salt, pepper, then one hen and one goat were killed, all of these things were put in a part of the coffin, for the uses of the rich man having reached the heaven. Having filled the juju-bag with some of his money, they hung it on the left shoulder of Simbi and it was this money he would be spending in the heaven. They explained to Simbi "You are now following your master to heaven and as you were a slave girl to him when he was alive thus you shall be for him in heaven. Therefore you must be taking great care of him. Be preparing his food at the right time. All his jujus and some of his properties are in the bag."

Having explained like that to Simbi, willing or not she was laid inside the coffin. She struggled very hardly to come out of it when the lid was nailing, but all her efforts were failed.

After, six strong men put the coffin on heads and the rest people were singing and following them to the river. Then the coffin was thrown in the river, and her master was buried at the bank of that river. Having done all these things they came back to the town.

And the coffin was floating along to where the water was flowing along. She was trying all her power just to break the coffin and come out, but she could not do it. Although she was lucky that some fresh air was blowing to the inside of the coffin, otherwise she should had died within two hours that she was inside it.

The water carried the coffin for many days before it carried it to its bank where there was no strong tide that could carry it further. This bank was near a big town.

A number of the fishermen of that town discovered the coffin at mid night, and they took it to the town. They thought that it was a box which contained precious things and that perhaps it fell from a canoe into the river by a mistake.

CHAPTER FOUR

The Life of Simbi in the Sinners' Town

When these fishermen opened the coffin they discovered that it were Simbi and her master's belongings were there. They were greatly terrified and then covered it back at once, because they thought Simbi was dead before she was put inside it.

"It will be better if we return this coffin to the river before morning, otherwise the guardsmen will arrest us for it," one of them suggested.

Then some of them put it on heads and the rest were following them to the river. Having travelled to the centre of the town, a number of the guardsmen who were on night duty challenged them. Instead to wait and explain how it was found, they threw it down and the whole of them escaped for fear of not being arrested.

And this coffin was carried to the king by the guardsmen. When its lid was removed before the king and his chiefs, they were greatly feared and were wondered greatly to see a girl (Simbi) put inside a coffin alive.

They took her out of it and asked who had put her there, but she was unable to answer because she was half dead at that time. But after a while, when the fresh air rushed to her, she explained to the king how she was put there. Then he (king) ordered his people to give her food and water. He said to himself that if he could treat her and could become healthy, she would be among of the slaves who were to be sacrificed to his head when it was time. Because this king used to sacrifice more than two thousand slaves to his head every year, so that he might live longer. And the sacrifice was taking place before his gods which were in a special built shrine.

Then Simbi became a slave again and she was put among the slave girls whom the king had bought before her. She was working with them and they were awaiting for the time that the king would sacrifice them on presence of his gods to his head.

Only sinners were living in this town. They were pagan. They were not sacrificing neither fowls nor animals to their gods but their slaves.

Simbi was greatly surprised when she met her four friends among the slaves. They were Rali, Sala, Bako and Kadara. But Rali and Sala had just been kidnapped before her. Bako and Kadara had been kidnapped since when they were children.

All of them embraced Simbi with gladness when they saw her. Then she asked "How did all of you manage to be in this town as well?" "We were kidnapped from our village and brought here by Dogo," her friends explained with sorrow.

"And I too were kidnapped from the junction near our village by the same Dogo, and he sold me in a town where

I was put inside the coffin and thrown it in the river," Simbi explained.

"I am afraid, Dogo will nearly kidnap all the children to this town," Bako wondered.

"How was my twin sister before you left our village, Simbi?" Bako asked, because she was a twin and her second was with her mother.

"Your twin sister and your mother were in good condition before I left the village but they were still in deep grief for your loss," Simbi replied.

"But I wonder, how Dogo managed to kidnap you from your wealthy mother, Simbi?" Rali asked. "Oh yes, thank you very much for asking me the reason. You see, when I had become tired of my mother's wealths and had fed up with the enjoyments and freedom that the wealths had been giving me, I told my mother that I liked to know the 'Poverty' and the 'Punishment' and to experience their difficulties. But when she refused to tell me the meanings of the two words, then I made the sacrifice which could help me to know them, and when I took it to the junction Dogo kidnapped me from there."

Rali and the others exclaimed when Simbi explained of what she was finding about. They blamed her seriously for it. But they were happy to see each other again.

Though all of them were working hardly every day for the king, their buyer, but he was not giving them anything to eat for many days, because he recognised them as goats.

"Yay—ay! punishment and poverty are too severe beyond of what a young girl like myself should try to experience. Of course, I had already been warned by my mother not to try to know them," Simbi remarked painfully one day when she and her friends were nearly punished to death by the king.

"Oh—o! which means you had already been warned not to try to know the 'Poverty' and the 'Punishment'?" Bako asked wonderfully. "Oh yes," Simbi replied sorrowfully. "And which means you had fed up with all the happinesses, merriments, etc. that which the wealths of your mother had been giving you?" Kadara asked with astonishment.

"Of course, but I have found out now my silly mistake," Simbi responded.

"Surely, Simbi, you have already found with your hands for yourself the everlasting poverty and punishment!" Sala added when she remembered with mind all the wealths of Simbi's mother.

"I admit," Simbi replied seriously.

"Put in mind that all of us are going to sacrifice to the king's head in the very near future," Rali reminded her.

"What is the remedy now, I mean how can I free from all these punishments?" Simbi asked calmly from Rali.

"Remedy?" Rali astonished. "Yes," she muttered.

"Let me tell you now, Simbi, there is no remedy at all in this Sinners' town. You have already involved yourself in punishment, poverty, etc. And this is to remind you that a person who has already fallen in water, there is no need for the person to run for the cold any more hence your mother is wealthy and you have fed up with her wealths, but you have preferred the poverty and punish-

33

ment most. Therefore, there is no need to fear for anything which may happen to you," Kadara explained briefly.

Having heard like that, Simbi sighed and then remarked painfully "It is hopeless for me then."

Then all of them continued to work. Thus Simbi and her four friends, Rali, Sala, Bako and Kadara and with about ten slave girls whom the king had bought before them, were working hardly every day without sufficient food, till they had completed one year.

When the day that the king would sacrifice them to his head remained five days, he gathered all his dirty clothes together, he gave them to them for washing. For it were these clothes he was going to wear in the night that he would sacrifice to his head. Because if he did not wear such clean clothes as these in that night his head would not accept the sacrifice and by that the head would not help him to live longer. And whenever his clothes were given to his slaves for washing, it meant that his sacrificial day was approaching and all of his slaves should be getting ready to die.

When the day reached, the king's guardsmen took all his slave girls to the outside of the town where the shrine of his gods was built. Simbi, Rali, Sala, Bako and Kadara were among the other slave girls whom were taken to the shrine. This shrine faced the Path of Death.

There were twelve tall trees at the front of the shrine. Then each of them was tied with rope to each of the trees. All of them faced the shrine. After that the door of the shrine was opened very wide. Both inside and outside of it were swept very clean. All the fearful gods which occupied the shrine were dressed with the new or green palm fronds.

Several long palm fronds were hung at the entrance of the shrine and that was a door blind. After that the surroundings were dashed with plenty of the palm fronds, just to show the people that the king would sacrifice to his head in the mid-night of that day.

Having done all of that, they (guardsmen) dressed all the slaves with the palm fronds and with a kind of the leaves which were very hot if touched the body. And all of them started to cry loudly immediately they covered them with these hot leaves. All of them became mad at the same time.

After a while, women and men of the town came there when they were hearing their cry which was a sign for them that the decorations were completed. And that was the reason why the hot leaves were for their last decoration.

Then the women were dancing and singing round them while those guardsmen were busy in sharping their swords.

Those women did not stop of singing and dancing round and round and round till when the king, chiefs and the prominent people arrived there in the mid-night. Then those women went back to the town, for having seen the king and others they believed that it was the time for the sacrifice, and that must not happen on the presence of women, that was forbidden.

When the king and the others (chiefs and prominent people of the town) entered inside the shrine and sat down before the gods, the slaves were loosened from the trees and then were taken by the guardsmen to the inside of the shrine and they were forced to kneel down before the gods.

After that colas were split, palm oil was poured on the heads of the gods. Then the king held the split colas with both his palms which were secured together. He touched his head with the split colas for three times. After that he opened the palms widely, he showed the colas to the whole gods and asked from them "Pay heed to my prayers now and let all what I say before you this mid night be so. Those who are before you now are the twelve slave girls that I bring for you. [He showed the twelve slave girls to the gods.] Let me reign longer and live longer than my predecessor, and be helping me to get the slaves always. But now, if you accept my prayers and that you are happy to accept these twelve slave girls, let the faces of half of these split colas face the ground."

Having said all his prayers, he threw down the split colas before the gods. But to his greatest horror and surprise, it were only three of the whole split colas faced the ground, the rest faced up. Having seen this, he was excited with the great fear and was nearly run mad at the same moment. Because as it were only three of the split colas faced the ground. It meant his gods and head did not accept his prayers, and it meant that a very bad omen was ahead, probably he was going to die in a few minutes time. And he threw down all the split colas for the second and the third times but it were only three of the split colas faced the ground as the first time.

Having seen this again, he was so puzzled at the same time that he was staggering about in the shrine. Although all the chiefs and the prominent people who were in the shrine with him guided him not to run out of the shrine, because they thought that he had already mad.

A few minutes later, he became conscious, then he came back and stood before his gods. But he was not happy at all. For if it were half of the split colas faced the ground and the rest half faced up, then it meant the gods and his head accepted his prayers.

"What is the next thing to be done now, for I believe, that I have bad omen for this year?" he asked from the chiefs and the prominent people with embarrassment.

"Yes, the next thing to be done now, is to start to behead these twelve slave girls and to be pouring their blood onto the gods. Perhaps if we do that, your (king) head and your gods will accept your prayers at that time," they advised him.

Then the king forced all the slaves to sing the song with which to behead everyone of them. Because everyone of them must form a kind of a song and when singing it nearly to the end, then the king himself would behead her with a sword.

Willing or not the first slave at the extreme right formed a kind of a song at the same time. And when she was singing the song nearly to its end the king beheaded her and the chiefs and the prominent people took her body from the ground, they poured the blood of her neck onto the heads of the gods and onto the king's head as well. Thus the king was doing to everyone of the slaves until it was the turn of Simbi, before it would be the turn of Rali, Sala, Bako, Kadara and some of the other slaves who were not the natives of their village.

But as Simbi had been an expert singer in her village it was easier for her to form a kind of a long sorrowful song at the same time. And she was mentioning a part of the song often and often to the king—"Please, the king, set the rest of us free." "Ha!—a!—a! don't you know you have become the slave of these gods this mid night!" the king and the rest exclaimed at a time.

"Please, the chiefs, deliver us from these gods!"

"Ha!—a!—a! you chiefs, don't you hear her plead now!" the king exclaimed to the chiefs. Then the chiefs, king, the prominent people and with the whole of the common people who were at outside of the shrine replied to Simbi's request with song loudly—"Don't you hear, she asks the chiefs to deliver her. But she does not aware that she had become the slave of the gods this mid night, who (gods) are going to drink her (Simbi's) blood just one or two minutes time!"

Having heard like that, Simbi did not waste the time. She changed that song to a kind of a melodious song.

When she started to sing it, the king, the chiefs, the prominent people and the common people who were at the outside of the shrine had lost all their senses at the same time and then were dancing here and there and were shouting loudly with great joy.

As they were still dancing about, it was so Simbi was thinking in mind how she could be saved. "If I had obeyed my mother's warning, all these things would have not happened to me. Yay—ay! I am dying this mid-night! Of course, my spook may go and inform my mother that I have been killed for the gods of the Sinners' town," Simbi painfully said.

Accidentally, it came to Simbi's mind at that moment to grasp the sword which the king held, with which he had beheaded some of the slaves before her own turn.

"Hurah! hurah! hurah!" the king with the rest people exclaimed with happiness.

"I am happy now that my head and gods accept my sacrifice and accept all my prayers as well, if not so this slave (Simbi) will not be singing a melodious song as this one!" the king happily announced to his people.

When he and the chiefs, etc. danced back to the gods and as Simbi was laid down before them (gods) all the while, and immediately he (king) raised up the sword just to behead her as well as he had beheaded many others, she jumped up and grasped the sword from him. Without hesitation she beheaded him with that sword and some of the chiefs, etc. as well who attempted to hold her for killing. And the rest chiefs, the prominent people and all the common people who were dancing at the out-side of the shrine, having seen this, they were dis-ordered.

As the whole of them were still hurthing here and there, Simbi with the rest slaves who had been expecting their turn to die, ran out of the shrine. Having glanced round there for a shelter and when there was none, they were running along on a path that which was found thereabouts as hastily as they could, so that they might run far away and then shelter themselves from the people of the Sinners' town, who probably might be chasing them to kill.

But Simbi still held the sword with which she had beheaded the king, etc. Thus she saved herself and the rest slave girls of about nine in number, among of whom were Rali, Sala, Bako and Kadara respectively.

Having run furiously on that path for about one hour and became tired, then they started to walk along slowly. Having travelled till the daybreak but they did not reach a town and they did not meet anybody, then they stopped and sat down in form of a circle and were mobbed, of course, they were always on the alert perhaps the people of the Sinners' town were chasing them to kill.

CHAPTER FIVE

On the Path of Death

When they were quite sure that that path was the Path of Death, they thought first to return to the Sinners' town and from there to find out for a safe path on which to be travelling and looking for the right way to their village.

But then they remembered that the people of the Sinners' town would catch and kill them as a revenge of what they had done to them before they had escaped from the shrine. Therefore they did not attempt to go back and they did not go further but sat down on this Path of Death.

Having moped for some minutes, the first question that Simbi perplexly asked was "Am I now a spook, Bako, because I remember now that I had already been beheaded last mid-night by the king of the Sinners' town?" "Not at all, Simbi, you were not beheaded by anybody, but you were the brave girl who beheaded the king together with some of the chiefs, etc., and by so did, the rest of us were saved by you," Bako explained to her.

"All right, Bako, but I am not yet sure that I am not a spook!" The rest sighed and glanced at her whether she was mad.

41

"But as there was no any safe path on which to travel except this Path of Death, I am sure, all of us are going direct to the house of death and he (death) shall kill us without any struggle!" Rali thought, and the rest were terrified when heard this.

"But ladies, I want you to believe that we are now a gang of refugees!" Sala reminded the rest. "Surely, we believe before you remind us, that we are now refugees," the rest said. "What are we going to eat, because I am nearly to die now of hunger?" Simbi asked calmly. "Of course, you are our leader and you suppose to find what all of us shall eat," the rest replied.

Then Simbi stood up, she went round there for any edible thing, but there was none to be found, except a kind of a tree which had the fleshy props could be found. And she cut some of them with the sword with which she had killed the king of the Sinners' town. Then she brought them to her gang. These fleshy props were to be roasted in fire before they were to be eaten, but there was no fire. Having thought of the fire for a while, they raised up their heads, they looked round as far as their eyes could reach. Luckily a light smoke was rushing out on the summit of a mountain, and it was the fire which the eruptions had caused. And at the same time, two ladies went there and a few minutes after, they brought the fire. Then the dried refuses and sticks were gathered together and they put the fire in it, and within ten minutes, it became a big fire. The fleshy props were roasted and they ate them, and it was about eight o'clock, in the morning by that time.

On the Path of Death

Having satisfied their hunger with the fleshy props (roots), they sat round the fire, they were warming their bodies with it.

After a while, Simbi, the leader, suggested whether they could continue to be travelling along the on Path of Death, hence they could not go back to the Sinners' town, and they could not stay with the fire throughout their lives time.

"I suggest that it would be better if we should start from here to be finding the way to return to our village," Kadara suggested.

"But we ought to be travelling on a path probably before we can trace out the right path to our village!" Simbi exclaimed.

"And we are to put in mind that we have lost the right path to our village from the Sinners' town. And now we cannot trace out the right part of the world that our village is!" Rali reminded the rest loudly.

"Of course, I am quite sure, our village is at the West!" Sala said. "No! is at the north!" Bako doubted. "At the north? No! that is entirely wrong, please. But our village is at the east!" Kadara explained.

"All right, ladies, to make sure of which part of the globe that our village is, let us wait until the run rises. For I am quite sure, any part of the sky that the sun appears in the morning, is the west, and that is the part of our village is!" Simbi explained.

"Oh yes! that is a fair judgment!" Bako supported. "All right, let us be keeping watch of the time the sun will appear!" the rest confirmed.

43

On the Path of Death

Note: Bako, Rali, Sala, Kadara and Simbi were kidnapped by the same Dogo from the same village, although Simbi was kidnapped after the rest four were kidnapped. But the names and villages of the rest ladies were not known, because they had been kidnapped by the same Dogo from their villages since when they were children, although the whole of them were behaving towards each other as sisters after they had bolted away from the shrine of the Sinners' town. But Simbi was quite sure that Bako was a Siamese twin by birth, her second was a girl as well who was a very rough-mannered girl and she was with her (Bako's) mother in their village.

Then the whole of them stood up, they huddled quietly, rose up their heads to the sky and were waiting for the sun to appear. But unfortunately there was no trace of the sun from the sky, the day was murky.

A few minutes later, Bako remembered "But we are in the rainy season and sometimes the sun does not appear at its right position, and sometimes it will not appear at all for the whole of this day, or even for many days to come!" "Oh yes! you are right, Bako. We are in the rainy season, therefore we cannot wait for the sun to show us the direction of our village!" the rest supported.

"Now, ladies, what to do next!" one of the nameless refugees exclaimed.

"Let's throw some dust into the sky and to any direction the breeze blows it, that is the right direction that our village is," Sala suggested.

"Yes, that is another good idea!" the rest exclaimed and were agreed to do so.

On the Path of Death

Then they looked thereabout for the dust but there was none to be found, for every part of the ground was wet and muddy.

"Ladies! we have forgotten, we are in the rainy season and therefore we cannot get the dust from the ground except the wet heavy earth or mud!" Simbi reminded the rest and all of them grinned.

At this stage the whole refugees buried their heads under their arms, they kept quiet and were thinking as how to reach their respective villages and also as how they would not travel on this Path of Death before they would reach their villages.

After a while, Simbi, the leader, stood up unexpectedly, she walked round there. She took a handful wet earth from the ground and then came back to the fire, but the rest were looking at her and expecting what she was going to do with the wet earth. Then she dried it with the fire and it became a dust at once having pressed and rubbed it with both palms. Then with all her power she threw the dust into the sky. But alas! there was no powerful breeze at that moment which could blow it, and it came down only a few inches from them.

Having failed for this again, Kadara suggested "I am now quite sure, there was no strong breeze at this moment. But I suggest, if we cut one leaf and throw it into the sky, to any direction it flies is the west and that is the direction of our village!"

"Good! you are quite right, Kadara, and you are sensible too!" the rest praised her. And then Bako, the Siamese twin among them, went to a tree nearby, she cut

45

one leaf from it. With all her power she threw it into the sky. But to their greatest horror and disappointment, the only light air which was blowing at that moment, blew this leaf along the Path of Death, though they had rejected this path as a safe one. And a few seconds after, the strong breeze came and it started to blow everything along the Path of Death, and within that moment, the sun appeared from where the Path of Death went along.

Having seen all these things which were against their thought, the whole of them stood up, they muddled at a little distance from the fire. Then they gazed at the sun just to make sure of the right direction that it (sun) appeared. But still, they discovered that it appeared from the direction of the Path of Death. "Ladies, I don't feel that the direction to which the breeze is blowing everything now, is the west. Therefore I am not sure that this Path of Death goes to our village!" Simbi exclaimed painfully. "This Path of Death goes along to our village hence everything is blowing along there!" Bako replied.

"We are now confused by the sun and this breeze, because I believe that this Path of Death which these two things (sun and breeze) are pointing out to us now as the right path on which to be travelled to our village, is entirely false," Bako said softly.

"And I am quite sure, if we follow this Path of Death, the whole of us shall be perished in a few days' time!" Rali supported Bako.

"That means all of us are going to die here!" Sala said sharply.

"If we refuse to travel on this Path of Death, where

are we going to travel then? Hence the bush and forest are so thick, thorny, full up of the imps and with incalculable snakes, all of which had once driven us out to this Path of Death," Kadara explained.

At this stage, the rest shook up and down their heads heavily, thought over of the point that Kadara had just raised. A few minutes after, Simbi asked "Are we going to vanish or die here, hence we refuse to travel neither in the forest nor on this Path of Death?"

"Surely, one must be for us, either to die or vanish here," Sala said calmly.

"We have now come to the climax!" Rali said painfully. "Indeed!" the rest confirmed loudly.

BAKO, THE TERRIBLE SIAMESE TWIN

But to their greatest surprise was that immediately they concluded their arguments at about ten o'clock a.m. Bako, the Siamese twin, picked a long, round stone from the ground. She started to beat all of them and she beat Simbi severely more than the rest. For Bako was acting like a mad lady unexpectedly.

When they could no longer bear the beat and it was impossible for them to snatch the stone from her, then they were hurtling along the Path of Death without their wish and she was chasing them along and was still beating them. It was like that this gang of refugees continued to travel on this fearful path.

When Bako chased them till the night-fall she became tired. The rest had already tired before that time, but she did not allow them to stop and rest.

When she stopped and sat down, the rest did so. When they noticed that she became conscious, Rali asked softly from her "By the way, Bako, what had been wrong with you at the time you were beating us with stone?" Having heard this, she implored the gang first before she started to explain to them of what had been wrong with her. "As some of you are quite sure that I am a Siamese twin and you believe also that my second, who is a girl, is a Siamese twin as well, and as both of us were born the same minute, so as I had been treating you it was so my mother or somebody else had been treating her at home. As she had been feeling the pain of the beat, etc., it was so I too had been feeling the same pain here. Anything which may happen to her it must happen to me at the very moment wherever I may be. If she steals something at home thus I too will steal something. Therefore, I apologise for the future whenever I treat you roughly like the first time so that you must bear it without any complaint!" thus Bako, the Siamese twin, explained briefly to her gang.

When the rest heard this terrible explanation they winked to each other and then all sighed with grief at the same moment.

"But, Bako, I beg you that next time when you shall become mad again don't beat me more severe than the rest," Simbi warned Bako because she beat her severely more than the rest at the first time.

"Eh, don't complain about that, Simbi! Were you not telling us the other day when we were in the Sinners' town, that you left our village just to find out the

'Poverty' and 'Punishment' and then to experience their difficulties?" Bako asked simply.

"Of course, my wish before I left our village was to seek for the 'Poverty' and 'Punishment' but I have regretted it since when Dogo had just kidnapped me and sold me," Simbi explained coldly.

"But before you will regret your wish will be when you return to our village," Bako replied and then she asked sharply from the rest "or is it not so?" "Yes, it is so!" the rest confirmed loudly.

"Yay! this is another terrible punishment and this kind of the punishment is even more severe than the punishment of this Path of Death," Simbi mumbled.

It was on this path they slept till morning. But it was Bako's weeping woke the rest, for she had become a weeper before the dawn. She was weeping so loudly that a person from one mile off could hear her.

When the rest asked of what she was weeping for, she replied that her mother or somebody else was scoffing her Siamese twin sister at home and she (sister) was weeping at that very moment for the scoff.

Having discussed together of what they could eat and they never knew yet, Kadara stood up, she went round. Luckily she discovered plenty of mushrooms. She rooted them out of the ground and brought them to the rest. As they had no fire with which to cook the mushrooms before eating them, they scraped the dirt away from them. But when they were about to start to eat them with greediness, for they were nearly to die of hunger, at that very moment Bako started to knock everyone of them at

49

mouth, face, etc. She gave Simbi an extra heavy knock which made one of her (Simbi) teeth to fall out suddenly.

At last when they could no longer bear the knock, they left the mushrooms and started to travel along. Thus Bako did not let them eat the mushrooms.

After some hours she stopped to knock them and then she explained "You see, someone had been knocking my Siamese twin sister at home and when I too felt the pain of the knock here, that was the reason why I had been knocking all of you."

And then Simbi was weeping bitterly along the path for the pain of the tooth which Bako had knocked out by force from her mouth. It was so Bako was illtreating them along the path until she drove them to a wonderful town.

CHAPTER SIX

The Town of the Multi-Coloured People

Immediately they entered this town without their wish, they entered a big house and met an old womans at with sorrow in one of the rooms that were in that house. She was the owner of the house.

They hardly saluted her when they hurriedly begged her for the cold water with which to quench their thirst that which had nearly killed them, because that day was muggy.

The woman was greatly feared them having seen their horrible attitude and having noticed that they were mono-coloured persons, for she had never seen such the mono-coloured persons as these gang of refugees in her life. Anyhow, as she was a good natured old woman, she showed them the pot of water with her finger. She was se old that it was hardly for her even to stand and walk away from her seat and she was even poorer than a church rat, for she had no any issue or one who could feed her.

It was after they drank the water when they could notice that the whole people of this town and with their domestic animals were multi-coloured, and they were greatly wondered and feared in respect of this multi-colour and thus the old woman was looking at them with wonder and fear in respect of their own mono-colour as well.

Having rested for a few minutes on standing, because the woman did not tell them to sit, they told her to allow them to stay in her house for some days and then to continue their journey. "Where are you coming from and where are you going?" the old woman asked with the weary voice.

"We are just coming from the Sinners' town, and we are looking about for the right path which goes to our village and to go back," they explained with respect.

The old woman paused for a while, and then asked "On which path did you travel to this town?" "We travelled on Path of Death."

"On Path of Death? and you did not meet any danger on it before reaching this town?" the old woman nodded and then asked patiently. "Just so," they replied softly. The woman was greatly wondered to hear this, because there was no a person who could travel on Path of Death for two days without being killed by the noxious creatures.

"I am afraid of your mono-colour, anyhow, I shall have mercy on you to allow you to stay in my house, but I will show you to the king first who will permit me to do your request, because he will be the one who will punish you if you offend me in future," she explained quietly.

The whole people of the town were rushing out of their houses and were following them to the palace of the king as the old woman was taking them along. And the king was also terrified when he saw them with their mono-colour.

"On which path did you travel to this town?" the king asked this question as well with great wonder. But as Simbi, the leader, had the gift of the gab more than the rest of her gang, she replied very sharply, "We travelled on Path of Death hence there is no any other path after that."

"Hah!—a!—a! you travelled on Path of Death which belongs only to death, poverty, punishment, illness, cruel, etc., etc.!" the king together with his incalculable people that surrounded him exclaimed unexpectedly immediately they heard this explanation from Simbi.

Then the old woman told the king that they asked her to allow them to be staying in her house and she told him to approve the request of the refugees before she would allow them to stay. When she told the king like that, the whole people exclaimed "Not at all! we shall not allow you (refugees) to stay in our town, hence you are the mono-coloured persons and we are the multi-coloured people." And the king himself said sharply "We don't hate yourselves but your mono-colour." But he agreed when Simbi explained their difficulties which they had met in the past or before they came there. And he told them that everyone of them must find a kind of work a to be doing for her living, he told them that he did not want any thief in his town.

They thanked him greatly and then followed the old woman back to her house.

The Town of the Multi-Coloured People

She gave one room to each of them to be living in, because there were many rooms in that house. She told them that everyone must be feeding herself, and they agreed.

And everyone was earning her living, but Simbi being a lady of strong physique among the rest, she made a big farm at a little distance from the town. She planted many kinds of crops.

THE PUNISHMENT OF SIMBI IN THE TOWN OF THE MULTI-COLOURED PEOPLE

One day, when the crops were ripen, Simbi noticed that some animals were coming to the farm from a long distance and they were eating the crops. Having discovered this, she went round the bush which surrounded this farm and she discovered the path of those animals on which they were travelling to that farm.

But there was no other kind of a trap except to set the rope or to dig a deep pit at the centre of an animal's path. Therefore, Simbi dug a deep pit at the centre of the path of the animals. Though they were not animals as called but their appearances was just seemed so.

Three days after, Simbi went there. But she was greatly surprised to meet inside the pit three kinds of creatures. They were in the forms of tiger, snake, and a rat who was a hole dwelling animal respectively. And a hunter fell into the pit as well, by a mistake, in the midnight, when he was travelling on that path just to kill any animal he could find. This hunter was a native of the town of the multi-coloured people.

The Town of the Multi-Coloured People

All the three animals and the hunter were unable to come out of the pit. Having seen all of them there Simbi wanted to pull the hunter alone out as he was a person like herself, though he was multi-coloured person, and after that to kill those evil spirits who were changing to that of bush animals whenever they were going to the farm.

But as she was trying to pull him out, those animals explained as if they were persons, "Because this hunter is a person like yourself, therefore you are trying now to safe him alone among us. Perhaps he may be one who will cause your death in future."

"So the more you safe him out, the more you will safe us out as well, though we are bush animals," they persuaded Simbi just to think that they were animals. "Please don't mind them, they are bush animals, just take me out and after that I will shoot them to death for you," the hunter said hurriedly, because he too thought they were bush animals.

But Simbi was afraid indeed to take out only that hunter, when the animals insisted that unless if she would take them out as well. She paused for a few minutes with fear, and she was thinking of what to do next to safe the hunter alone.

A few minutes after, she remembered to ask the hunter of what he would do for her if she helped him out of the pit. For she thought as those animals were not human, they would not be able to make any promise, and for that reason, she would free from their blame if she took out only the hunter.

"Listen to me, my dear hunter, what kind of a help you will render to me if I take you out now?" Simbi asked from the hunter.

"You see, Simbi, the promise that I can give you now is that as from this day, I shall be keeping watch of your farm just to safe the crops from the animals which are eating them."

"Yes, tiger, what is your own promise?" she asked boldly. "As from this day, I shall be killing one bush animal every night and bringing it to the farm. Therefore, try to be going to the farm every morning to take the animal," tiger promised loudly.

"Yes, rat, what is your own promise?" "You see, I am a hole dwelling animal who can dig a parallel hole under the ground to a distance of twenty miles. Therefore I promise now that in a few days' time I shall dig such a hole from your room to the property room of the King of the multi-coloured people's town. I will pass all the king's properties, as gold, jewels, clothes, etc. from that property room through the hole to your room," the rat promised.

"Yes, snake, what is your own promise?" "I cannot tell you now the kind of my own promise. The reason is that some of the persons are kittle cattle and perhaps this hunter who is only a human among us inside this pit, may be one of the kittle cattle persons and he may be in future laid you heart bared.

"But in the indirect way, I heartly promise now that any day it is difficult for you, believe me, wherever you may be, I will come there just to fulfil my promise or to render my help to you," snake promised calmly.

After everyone of these victims had promised Simbi and everyone heard each other's promise except snake's promise which was indirect and the rest did not understand it.

Then Simbi took them out of the pit and everyone went to his own way. But when Simbi went to her farm in the following morning, she was greatly surprised to meet there one animal, which had been killed and had brought there by tiger, as he had promised. And the hunter fulfilled his own promise as well for he was keeping watch of the farm so that the animals might not eat the crops.

A few weeks later, the rat, as called, who was the hole dwelling animal, dug a parallel hole under the ground from Simbi's room to the inside room in which all the properties of the king were kept. Then he packed all the properties therein and brought them through the hole to her room.

But it remained only snake, as called, to fulfil his own indirect promise which Simbi never understand.

A few months later from when the properties of the king had brought to her room by the hole dwelling animal, rat, as called, one day, when the king wanted to go somewhere, he opened the door of his property room just to take some of the gold, etc., that which he wanted to wear to the place that he wanted to go.

In the first instance, he could not believe his eyes when he found none of his properties inside the room. His family rushed to the room when they heard him horribly exclaimed "Where are my properties! Who had done this?" he asked painfully from his family. "It should be a number of burglaries who had carried away the properties," his people were puzzled.

"I wonder, the windows or the door were not broken and there is no any sign which can show that the properties were carried away by the thieves," the king doubted. "Let us look at the partitions perhaps there·may be a sign which will show that the properties were packed out through there," one of the king's family advised.

The king hardly heard this advice to the end when he drew a three legged powerless stool near the window and off he climbed from the stool onto the partition. And hardly reached the partition when he fell headlong onto the floor and then he fainted. "Eh! the king falls and faints!" his family exclaimed until he became conscious. Then with pain he staggered back to his throne.

"But it is very disgraceful to a king like you to climb the partition for yourself in looking for something! If you don't respect yourself you must respect your office!" his prince who just heard and came in warned him painfully.

"The best thing which your majesty should have done, instead of climbing the partition for yourself, is to give the order to one of your bellringers, to announce what has happened with bell to everywhere in the town, perhaps some one may know one who has stolen the properties and then to bring the news to you," a young lady advised the king.

"Oh yes! you are right, lady, and it is today I believe that one person can never have the whole senses of this world. Thank you, lady! All right, call me one of my bellringers!" the king ordered. "Here I am, your majesty," the bellringer prostrated with face turned to the floor and was expecting what order the king would give. Neither to behead him or to send him to somewhere, he never knew which was which.

"Bring me my long smoking pipe!" the king ordered another man while the bellringer was still prostrated in his front.

When the pipe was brought, the man loaded it with newly withered tobacco and then plenty of hot-red coals (fire) were taken from the nearby heath and put them into the pipe.

It was this kind of a long pipe the king used to smoke in the day that a serious thing happened to him, or the day when an offender was to be beheaded before him or the day he had to sacrifice human to his gods, etc. But as he was too perplexed by the loss of his properties, so that he was unable to blow out the smoke from the pipe. "Please help me to blow out with your mouth the first smoke!" he ordered one of his chiefs. But about four chiefs grabbed the pipe from his mouth at a time, of course the rest left it for one of them at last.

He put it in the mouth and blew out the first thick smoke. After that he replaced it to the king's mouth. Then four of them (chiefs) held the rest part of the pipe while he was enjoying the smoking. Because this pipe was too heavy for the smoker to hold it for himself. Then the rest chiefs or those who stood round were blowing the air onto him with the woven large fans while the bellringer was still prostrated.

"Yes, my chiefs, which is the right message to send the

bellringer that which he is to deliver to the people of the town?" the king asked. "He is to announce with the bell for the people about your majesty's stolen properties," the chiefs explained. "Thank god, I think I am called to be sacrificed to the god but it is only to ring the bell," the bellringer gladly remarked having gone out of the palace.

Then he rang the bell to every part of the town. He announced to the people that any one who might know whereabouts the stolen properties should report to the king.

But because the hunter who was among those animals (as called), who had been fallen into the pit and had been saved out together with the animals the other day by Simbi, the owner of the pit, had heard when rat, the hole dwelling animal, was promising Simbi on that day that he (rat) would bring all the king's properties through the under ground hole to her room, and because this hunter had since then kept in mind the promise made by rat, therefore, immediately he heard the bellringer announce the stolen properties, he went to the king as a liar. He explained to him that all his properties were in Simbi's room. And without hesitation, the king sent a large number of guardsmen to her room.

Then they arrested her and took the properties and herself to the king. Without asking her how the properties came to her room, he ordered his guardsmen to tie her with a rope to the big tree which was at the front of the palace, ready to be killed to the gods in three days' time, at the presence of all the town's people.

There were many gods under this tree and several thousands thieves, wrong doers or offenders or those who had no even an offence had been sacrificed to those gods.

Having seen Simbi tied to the tree, both adults and children of the town came there. They were stoning at her, flogging and slapping her. Within one hour every part of her body was bleeding, she begged them with sorrowful voice, but they did not listen to her, and it was after she fainted of pains before they went back to their houses. Thus Simbi remained unconscious till the third night that she would be sacrificed to the gods.

When it was twelve o'clock of the third night, the pains were so much that she started to blame herself. "Hah! if I had obeyed my mother's warnings not to try to know the poverty and the punishment, all these should have not happened to me."

Luckily as she was still blaming herself like that, she perceived a snake at a long distance. Within that moment this snake changed to the gnome and he came to her. She did not know that the snake which she had saved out of the pit the other day was a gnome and not a snake.

At the same time, the gnome reminded her "This is a critical night for you and I come to fulfil my promise this night. And that was the reason I did promise you indirect the other day, because of that hunter who has put you now in this trouble. Do you remember that you have saved him from the pit the other day?" "Yes I remember," Simbi said calmly. "But he is going to cause your death now." "Anyhow, take this juju-powder, it can wake a dead person." "At all costs when it is one o'clock this mid night, the princess of the king will die unexpectedly. Whenever you hear the king and his family that they are weeping, tell anyone of them who comes out at that time, that you can wake the princess from dead, if the king can manage to get the head of a hunter who is also a liar.

"When the king brings it, then you will mix this juju-powder with the blood of that head. After that you will put the mixture into both eyes of the dead princess. Doubtless, she will wake up from dead at once. By so safe her, her father, the king, will not kill you for the offence, but set you free.

"And as that hunter is the only a hunter and a liar in this town, and as the head of a hunter who is also a liar must be brought to you before you can wake the princess, I believe that the hunter must be the right man in this town whose head will be available. Therefore the king will behead him, and bring his head to you to be used."

After the gnome had explained like that to Simbi, he gave her the juju-powder, after that he caressed her head and then he disappeared. Simbi was even healthier than ever immediately the gnome caressed her head, all the pains and bruises were vanished at once.

As a matter of fact, when it was one o'clock mid night, Simbi heard the king and his family were weeping bitterly. When she asked for the cause from a man who was passing near the tree to which she was tied, the man replied that the princess had just stopped the last breath.

"Has she been ill for a long time?" "Not at all!" the man replied painfully. "But if the king can get the head of a hunter, who is a liar as well, I will wake up the princess from the dead, because I have such a power." "Is that so?" the man wondered. "Yes, indeed!"

At the same time the man ran to the palace he repeated of what Simbi had told him to the king. And the king himself ran out of the palace. He hurriedly asked her of what she had told the man and she repeated it. Then he loosened the rope away from her body and without hesitation he held her left hand in a lovely way, he took her to the room in which the dead body of the princess was laid and ready for burial.

At the same time he gave the order to his statesmen to print a notice "THE HEAD OF A HUNTER WANTED! and they did so and pasted them to every wall and tree.

Within one hour that the notice had been pasted a man having read it came to the king. He reminded him about the hunter, who had told the king that his properties were in Simbi's room.

Immediately he heard this from that man, he sent four of his guardsmen to go and bring the head of the hunter. When the head was brought, Simbi mixed its blood with the juju-powder which the gnome gave her. Then she put the mixture into both eyes of the dead princess. And to the king's and his family's greatest surprise, the princess woke from the dead at once.

For the great admiration the king had on her marvellous work, he set her free. After that she came back to her room with happiness.

The hunter wanted the king to kill Simbi, but he died instead.

BAKO, THE SIAMESE TWIN, BECAME A COCK

Then Simbi and her gang were enjoying their lives and they had forgotten all their punishments of the past.

But Bako, the Siamese twin, was always stealing goats, rams, cocks, etc. from the town. If the rest cautioned her she would not agree. She would tell them that it was so her Siamese twin sister was stealing goats, etc. at home. The people of the town suspected that their animals were missing in great number every day, but they did not understand how they were missing.

As the old woman who was the owner of the house in which they were living, had one hen that which had six chickens at that time, and as Bako had seen this hen, she did nothing more than to be keeping watch of its movement, just to steal it.

A few days later, when Simbi had just freed from her trouble, one evening, when Bako noticed that the old woman, their landlady, had gone to somewhere, she went to the corner where their landlady's hen and its six chickens were scratching the ground for their food. She looked thereabout perhaps somebody might be near. When she was quite sure that there was nobody near, then she threw some corn on the ground from the hen to her room. When she saw the hen started to eat the corn with greed towards her room, then she hid herself at the back of the door of that room.

When the hen and its six chickens were swallowing the corn until they entered her room un-noticed, she shut the door while the hen and its chickens were inside the room.

The Town of the Multi-Coloured People

Without hesitation she caught them and killed them. After that she roasted them and kept them inside the cupboard ready for the mid night when she would eat them. Of course, the rest did not see her as she was playing this trick.

Within two hours from when she had roasted them the old woman came back from where she had gone to. But when she noticed that her hen and its chickens did not return home and they had never kept very long like that from outside, having struggled before she could stand up from the seat, she went round that area, she was calling them, but she did not see them at all. Then she was announcing loudly and sorrowfully "If my hen with its six chickens entered your house by a mistake, please tell me and I will come and take them back to my house!" But there was nobody answer, because all the people of that area and the rest refugees did not know anything about the hen, except Bako who stole them. She sat at the outside of the house by that time and she was looking at the old woman as how she was hurriedly going from house to house. Even she was sympathising with this old woman as if she was not the one who stole them and she was also cursing: "A very bad revenge and woe shall come unto one who has seen you as old and weary as this and then stole your hen on whose only chickens you are living."

At last when the poor old woman believed that the hen and its chickens could not be found and that somebody had stolen them, she cursed loudly, "Anyone who has stolen my hen shall become like that of the very hen before tomorrow morning. Everybody will see him or her in the plumage that my hen possessed and its six chickens will be following him or her about. And if there is god almighty, this my curse shall come to effect!"

Having cursed like that with sorrowful voice, she went back to her house. She was mourning the stolen hen as if it was a dead person, for she had nothing more than this hen in her life and she had no one who could be feeding her.

And as she had cursed like that, truly speaking! before five o'clock early in the morning, Bako's head had already changed into the cock's head and with a very big comb on this head and with a very big and long beak. Everyone of these changes was bigger than those every cock could possess. Every part of Bako's body was full of soft and strong feathers and it wondered everyone greatly as how all the feathers which she had pulled away from the dead body of the hen managed to grow again on her body.

The very brass ring that which the old woman had put in the left leg of the hen, which was the mark of distinction from other hens, was in the left ankle of Bako as well. Both her shoulders and arms were full of strong wings and all were belonged to that hen which she had killed and roasted.

Even Simbi and the rest refugees remarked in that morning "Hah! this is too wonderful and too terrible to be seen for both adults and children!" Because as the old woman had cursed in the evening, it was not yet five o'clock in the morning when Bako was crowing repeatedly with the voice that which was louder and more huge that an ordinary cock's voice should be. Her crow was hearing continuously from the dark corner of the room in which she hid for her fearful appearance. Of course, there was nobody noticed in the first instance that it was from her room the crow of cock was hearing.

But when it was eight o'clock and when the rest refugees noticed that she had not come out from her room, except the cock's crow that was hearing from there, then Simbi forced open the door of her room. She entered inside it. But she ran back to the verandah with great horror immediately she entered and saw her in this fearful appearance. And when Simbi was so much surprised that she did not know what to do, she ran to the outside of the house and then she cried loudly to the whole multi-coloured people of that area.

Within two seconds, that place had full of people. When some of the brave men entered the room and met Bako in the form of a cock they were nearly frightened to death. But anyhow they dragged her to the outside. And the rest people were greatly shocked with fear when they saw her terrible form, and all were exclaiming at the same time "Hah! this is first of its kind! We have never seen this in our lives!"

Within a few seconds that those people and the rest refugees were still exclaiming like that the news had reached everywhere in the town and to the king as well, as such a terrible news as this was travelling even quicker than the air to everywhere without being published. And within two or three minutes, two of the king's guardsmen arrived. They said that the king sent them to come and bring this cockish lady (Bako) to the palace.

To everyone's horror, as she was escorting along to the palace, all the six chickens which she had already killed and roasted together with their mother, were following her and crying continuously as if she was their mother, although she had already changed to their mother. Immediately she was escorted to the centre of the town the whole people saw her and they were hurthing here and there just to see her. And to their fear, whenever this cockish lady saw a hen, she was doing to that hen exactly as a cock was doing whenever it saw a hen.

Having taken her to the palace, she stood before the king and his councillors, and Simbi with the rest refugees stood behind her, they were expecting what the king would say, for they could not leave her and escape.

"How did you manage to change into this fearful form of a cock?" the king asked with astonishment. "Kokoroko-o! Koko-roko-o! Kokoroko-o-o!" Instead of explain herself to the king, she was simply crowing loudly and continuously like the cock of three years of age.

Having failed to explain herself and because she was too terrible to be seen for the king and his councillors and to the common people of the town, then the king told his councillors "If a man keeps too long in looking at this cockish lady, probably that man will change into the same form of a cock!"

Having announced like that, without hesitation he and his councillors were preparing to leave the town. But when the king together with his councillors, all of whom were responsible for the town, were leaving the town in respect of Bako, the cockish lady, what more for the common people of the town? But the right thing for the common people to do was to leave the town as well with their king, etc.

Then the whole people were following the king, etc. the rest refugees and the cockish lady also were following them, whereas they were leaving the town for her and then to hide themselves in another town. And to their disappointment, was that as they were reaching every town just to take a shelter from there, if the inhabitants of that town saw them together with Bako in the form of the cock, they were not allowing them to stay in their town. Thus they were driving them away from all the towns and villages that they reached.

At last they rushed to a bush, they hid themselves there, but at all costs Bako traced them out.

After a few days that they were in that bush, one of the king's advisers prostrated before the king and his councillors. He advised the king to make enquiries from the common people, if the cockish lady had offended one of them who had cursed her to become like that of a cock. The king with his councillors thanked this adviser greatly for the helpful advice which he had brought.

Then the king announced to the common people whether the cockish lady offended one of them. Luckily as many of these common people who were living near to the old woman's house, the owner of the hen, were among them and they had overheard when the old woman had been cursing one who had stolen her hen therefore, they explained that they heard when the old woman had cursed one who had stolen her hen to

69

become like that of her hen. They explained further that they could not definitely say whether Bako was the right lady who had stolen the hen. Although she changed into the cock instead of a hen as the woman had cursed, thus the people explained.

Without hesitation, the king sent two men to go and carry the old woman to him. They carried her by head to the king, because she was too old and weary to walk for herself.

Then he asked whether she was the right old woman who had cursed Bako to become like that of a cock. She replied at once that she did not curse anybody direct, but she cursed one who might had been stolen her hen with its six chickens.

The whole people were very sorry for this old woman having seen as she was very old, weary and helpless and they were greatly surprised also to see a young lady like Bako steal her hen or to see anyone who could steal anything which might belong to this old woman, who was extremely reched. At the same time, many of the people contributed a large amount of money, they gave it to the old woman. "By the way, why did you steal the hen?" the king asked painfully.

"It is not my fault at all to do so. I shall be grateful if His Majesty the king will listen to my explanations. I am a Siamese twin and my second is now in my village. So whenever she steals anything in my village, I will feel it at the same moment she steals the thing wherever I may be, and at the same time I will steal the same kind of the thing that which she steals. And this is the reason why

The Town of the Multi-Coloured People

I stole the old woman's hen and that means my Siamese twin sister stole a hen in my village!" Bako explained loudly to the king, etc. "Terrible!" the king and others exclaimed. "As the spirit of your Siamese twin sister had forced you to steal another person's property, it is so it will force you to die!"

"Escort her and the rest refugees into my shrine and I shall sacrifice them to my gods when it is mid-night, because I believe all of them are thieves!" the king gave order to his guardsmen. But he hardly explained like that when the rest refugees took to their heels, they entered into another bush, and Bako followed them in that form of a cock. The guardsmen chased them to catch, but when they could not overtake them, they shot many of the nameless refugees to death before they came back to their king.

Thus Simbi, Rali, Sala, Kadara, Bako who was the cockish lady and the rest of the nameless refugees who were not killed, left the town of the multi-coloured people, but Bako was still in the form of a cock, and Simbi was unable to take her sword along with her. It was that sword with which she had beheaded the king of the Sinners' town.

CHAPTER SEVEN

Simbi fought with the Satyr of the Dark Jungle

Then they continued their journey from one forest to another. And it was so Bako, the cockish lady, was crowing continuously and following them. When the troubles which she was giving them were unbearable, they scattered into the forest, just to safe themselves from her. At last Simbi and Rali escaped to one place, Sala, Kadara and the rest nameless refugees escaped to another direction, but after a while Bako traced them out and she was chasing them along at the same time.

When Simbi and Rali had travelled for two days with great fear for not being killed by unmentionable harmful living creatures of the forest, they came to the Path of Death, and having travelled on this fearful path for some hours they came to a jungle at one o'clock of the day, and without hesitation they started to travel along in this jungle.

After a while they travelled to a part of this jungle which was entirely dark. And having travelled further they were swallowed by the darkness. They could not even see each other at all. In respect of this, Simbi who was at the front held Rali's left hand so that they might not lose each other. It was like that they were dragging themselves along with fear until they saw a dreadful creature at a short distance from them. This creature stood firmly at the centre of this Path of Death.

This fearful creature was the Satyr of this Dark Jungle.

But Simbi and Rali stopped immediately they saw him in the darkness, and he saw them as well through his eyes which illuminated to every part of that spot immediately he goggled both eyes.

This Satyr was looking at them with these eyes that which showed he was nearly to die of hunger and then saw what he could eat unexpectedly.

"We are perished today," Rali said softly with her heart which was throbbing with fear.

"Of course," Simbi replied quietly with fear. "Are we to be going along or to return to where we are coming from?" Rali asked. "You know, Rali, it is impossible for us to go back or if we do so, the multi-coloured people will kill us," Simbi explained calmly. "What is to be done next then?" Rali asked.

But as they were still suggesting of what to do the Satyr shouted greatly with his horrible voice "Come along, my meat, I am ready to eat both of you now! Come along, and don't waste my time!"

At that moment their bodies were withered for fear, they could not move to either front or back and they were unable to talk out at all. When he had tired of waiting for them to come to him he was coming to them. When he approached them, they noticed that he did not wear

73

neither coat nor trousers but he wore only an apron which was soaked with blood. Plenty of the soft feathers were stuck onto this apron. More than one thousand heads of birds were stuck to all over it. He was about ten feet tall and very strong, bold and vigorous. His head was full of dirty long hairs and the hairs were full up with refuses and dried leaves. The mouth was so large and wide that it almost covered the nose. The eyes were so fearful that a person could not be able to look at them for two times, especially the powerful illumination they were bringing out always. He wore plenty of juju-beads round his neck. The spider's webs were spread over his mouth and this showed that he had not eaten for a long time. This Satyr was a pessimist, he was impatient and ill-tempered, impenitent and noxious creature. His beard was so long and bushy that it was touching the ground and he was using it for sweeping his house as if it was a broom. In respect of all these things, the king of this Dark Jungle appointed him as the guard of the jungle, and this Dark Jungle itself was the home of imps, gnomes, goblins and all other kinds of the evil spirits and there was a bold phoenix which was always flying to everywhere in this jungle, it was swallowing all kinds of other creatures which were coming there. And it was also appointed by the king to be an assistance for the Satyr.

This Satyr was always with a bunch of cudgels on head and one club of bone in hand. He was all the time carrying all these things about in the jungle.

When he was at a distance of about ten feet from Simbi and Rali, he stopped, he put the bunch of that cudgels down but he held the club of bone high and ready to beat them to death.

Then he started to ask with his powerful voice, "Who are you? What are you? where are you coming from? Where are going? or don't you know where you are? Answer me! I say answer me now!"

But Simbi and Rali could not answer at all, they were even hardly breathing at this critical moment. Their teeth were striking each other hastily with fear. Their eyes had already grown glassy and they could not say whether they were in heaven or on earth at that moment.

When they were unable to reply to all his questions, then he started to explain to them his terrible deeds. "Certainly, you have put yourselves into the mouth of 'death'! You have climbed the tree above its leaves! you see me coming and you too are coming to me instead to run away for your lives!

"By the way, have you not been told of my terrible deeds? And that I have killed and eaten so many persons, etc. who were even bold more than you do?

"My house is near this Path of Death and it is in this Dark Jungle this Path of Death is ended. And the poverties, punishments, difficulties, cruelties, etc. etc. are the rulers of this Jungle. Anybody who travels on Path of Death shall end his or her life in this jungle. I am the Satyr who is guiding this jungle since from two thousand years!

"But this day that you bring yourselves to me! Hah! having killed both of you, I shall enjoy your meat for a few days!

75

"Eh! are you going to sink into the ground or are you going to fly away? Although, you can safe yourselves from me if you have the power to do either one of the two things! Answer me now!"

When the Satyr had roared on them like that and before he could come nearer to beat them to death, Simbi started to flatter him, just to set herself and Rali free from this difficulty. Because as he was roaring on them he was gobbling the spit of his mouth as if he had already started to eat them. And they were greatly feared when heard all his sayings that they did not know what to say or do except to be flattering him and ask for pardon.

"Please, the Satyr, pardon us for all our mistakes to come here, and I believe all your sayings even before you explained yourself to us and I believe that there is no any person who will see you will not believe that you are a noxious Satyr," Simbi flattered him.

"You, ladies, believe me that the words 'beg' 'pardon' 'mercy' 'forgiveness' 'pity' etc. have been deleted from our language from a long time and I am the very one who had forced the king to do that and I forced the king as well to substitute the words 'sorrow' 'sufferance' etc. instead. And all these things had done by the king in respect of me for he knows that I cannot remain in any place that the words 'pity' 'beg' 'pardon' 'mercy' 'forgiveness' are ineffective!"

Having heard all of these again, Simbi and Rali were shrivelled with fear at the same time. Within that moment, Simbi had thought in mind "If a person is really going to die, he or she must struggle to the extreme end and I will do that, because I cannot remain quietly in one place till this Satyr will beat me to death."

Then she looked at him as if he was an ant and then she began to roar on him "Though I believe that you are the Satyr of this Dark Jungle and I do believe that you have killed and eaten several wayfarers or refugees like us!

"But to make it clear to you is that, refugees are quite different from refugees! Therefore I tell you now that if you insult us as well as you have done to others! Believe me! you will be one of the inhabitants of heaven today! And doubtless, you will dine with them today!" (All these sayings meant the Satyr would lose his life) "Let me explain in short to you now the Satyr, the noxious guard of the Dark Jungle. I am the daughter of the most wealthy woman in my village! I am the most beautiful girl in my village as well! I was a wonderful singer during the time that I was in my village. I have woken several deads with my song and I have killed many persons with my song as well! My song is a harmful charm which can kill a harmful and powerful Satyr like you within a few seconds.

"I proudly tell you now, that I left all my mother's wealths, I started to find about the poverties, punishments, sufferings, all kinds of sorrows, death, etc. Therefore, I am very glad to meet here what I am looking for and it is you. I am not afraid of your harmful deeds at all!

"I confess to you now that I have beheaded the king and some of the chiefs of the Sinners' town and I have

77

once been put in the coffin alive and the coffin was thrown in the river but my wonderful song saved me!

"Although, I believe that a powerful man but senseless is the father of sluggard, and a sluggard but sensible is a powerful man.

"I believe that you are a powerful Satyr but you are senseless, therefore all your powers are useless!

"I can change my song into any powerful creature now who can beat you to death at once. And I can change myself into 'Iro . . .' " (Iromi—a water insect.)

"Hah, don't leak out all what you can do to this Satyr, or don't you know that a lady never leaks out all her powers to her enemy as this Satyr," Rali cautioned Simbi not to leak out all she could do to the Satyr. And Simbi stopped at "Iro . . ." instead to mention the whole word "Iromi" which was the full word, immediately she heard the caution from Rali. And the Satyr was entirely confused about this word. He did not understand that it was abbreviated like that unexpectedly when Rali cautioned Simbi. Although the Satyr understood the meaning of "Iromi" as a water insect but he did not understand "Iro . . ." as "Iromi."

Having confused the Satyr about this word, Simbi started to say "Woe unto you, the Satyr, the noxious guard of the Dark Jungle! Woe unto you! I am ready now to fight with you!"

The Satyr was greatly feared when he heard all Simbi's boasts. He did not aware that Simbi was a braggart and that her boasts were not effective. Although the boasts had rendered his power absolutely useless, but still,

Simbi fought with the Satyr of the Dark Jungle

Simbi hardly finished her boasts when he gnashed and dashed to Simbi so heavily that she staggered to a few feet. And it was a scrimmage indeed.

In the first instance, the Satyr attempted to lift Simbi up and then to knock her onto a rock that was nearby, but she did not give him the chance to do that. And thus she attempted to do but all her efforts were failed. Because as she was struggling hardly it was so the Satyr himself was fighting her fiercely. His feet were shaking the trees that were near by as if they were going to fall down.

They held each other tightly and their eyes were opened so widely that they (eyes) nearly to tear like a cloth, and both were perspiring as if they were drenched by rain. After a while the Satyr jumped on Simbi's nape unexpectedly and he was pulling out the hairs of her head in large quantity. At this stage, Simbi felt much pain, she gnashed and she did not care for any consequences. She took him near to a very deep pond which was full up with water. While she was trying to throw him into that pond, Rali was beating him severely on the head with a heavy stone. But as he was trying to bend Simbi's head and then press it into the water of the pond so that she might drink the water to death, Rali gave him an extra heavy blow at the back suddenly. And in trying to come down from Simbi and then to revenge from Rali, unfortunately he fell headlong into the pond and he drowned at the same time.

Without hesitation Simbi and Rali were running away as fast as they could so that they might travel far off before he would come out from the pond.

"It was only the God almighty helped me to conquer this Satyr. Because I am not bold, strong and brave enough in any way to face him," Simbi told Rali with weak voice.

Having struggled for about thirty minutes the Satyr came out of the pond and he chased them at once, he wanted to kill them for his food. For it was a great disappointment to him to loose them. But all his efforts were failed, he could not trace them out any more. The ladies had travelled as far as to such a long distance that he could not see them.

"I believe, the two ladies shall come back to this jungle and I shall kill both of them at all costs at any day I meet them. It is certain, they are my meat! . . . By the way, what is the meaning of 'Iro . . .'? of course, I know the meaning of 'Iromi' that is an insect of water, but what of 'Iro . . .' into which that lady [Simbi] said she could change? Anyhow we shall meet again and then continue our fight!" the Satyr was saying like that when he was returning having failed to trace them out. And he was greatly feared and powerless especially when Simbi boasted that she had killed many persons with her song and the song could change into any harmful creature.

When they travelled very far in this Dark Jungle, they came to a flat rock. It was in an open place and it exposed to the sun. They stopped there. Hardly climbed it to the top when Simbi fell down and Rali sat closely to her. Simbi was so weak that she lay down helplessly as if she had dead. Because she had fought the Satyr beyond her power.

80

Simbi fought with the Satyr of the Dark Jungle

When it was about twenty minutes that Simbi had laid helplessly on that rock, and when Rali noticed that her condition did not improve well, she was puzzled. She thought perhaps Simbi was going to die. "How do you feel now?" Rali asked quietly. "There is no better improvement at all. Even I am feeling cold as well," Simbi muttered. "Feeling cold again?" Rali was greatly embarrassed when she heard like that from her. And she explained "Here is no fire with which to warm your body?"

"Of course, let us leave the matter of fire first. But how can we get something to eat, for I am feeling to eat badly?" Simbi asked seriously.

"I wonder, I don't know where to get food, and there is no any edible thing near this place," Rali explained.

"You may go round here, probably you may get some of edible fruits," Simbi advised calmly with sick voice.

Then Rali left her on that rock, she was going from one tree and then to another, she was looking for the edible fruits. Thus she was going on and on and no until she had travelled about one mile from the rock.

But a few minutes after she had left Simbi, a strange eagle was flying about. It was searching for the food which to be given to its nestlings. Its nestlings were on top of a high mighty tree. To top of this tree had been cut off by the strong wind from a long time. And its remaining stump was still about five hundred feet tall. It had a very huge hole which went zigzag from the top to the last tap root of it.

When this eagle discovered Simbi had noticed how she

lay down helplessly on the rock, it thought she was a dead animal. At the same time it pounced to her. It held her cloth and then flew up with her.

As it was flying away with her, Rali saw her with the eagle when she was just returning with the fruits she could find.

"Please Rali! please Rali! please Rali! come and take me back from this eagle! Please don't let this eagle take me away! Please snatch me back from it!" Simbi exclaimed hurriedly.

"Ah Simbi! ah Simbi! don't let the eagle take you away! Try to take yourself from it! Don't leave me alone in this jungle and go away!" Rali was greatly shocked.

Thus Simbi and Rali were crying loudly to each other until the eagle had carried her away. After the eagle vanished among trees and hills, Rali bursted into a great tear. Because there was nobody with whom to be discussing and to be travelling with. And she started to wander about in this Dark Jungle and she was weeping repeatedly for the loss of her friend, Simbi.

"If it were you or I how in deep grief you or I would be?"

Having wandered for about four months she discovered Kadara, Sala, the other nameless refugees and Bako, the Siamese twin who was still in the form of a cock, and then she was wandering about with them.

CHAPTER EIGHT

Simbi became the wife of the Woodcutter

When the eagle flew for a few minutes, it came to the tree on top of which its nestlings were in the nest. Then it threw Simbi down on the centre of the nest for its nestlings to eat her. But as she was heavier than what the nest could hold or stop, therefore she simply rolled from there down to the bottom of the hole, and luckily she had no any wound at all, for the smooth refuses prevented her from that.

Now, Simbi was at the bottom of the hole helplessly. She cried out for help till her voice had become entirely hoarse, but there was nobody who could drag her out.

After a while, she became conscious when the fresh air rushed to her from the top of that tree. Then she gathered all the refuses to one part of the hole. She sorted out all the fluffy ones. She spread them onto one place and it was just like a mattress. All these refuses were falling into the hole from the eagles, hawks, parrots, etc. which were living on top of the tree.

Then she lay flatly on this mattress of refuses, she faced up and she was looking at the sky far off through the

83

top of the tree. Her intention was that she would see something which would take her out. But she did not understand all what she was seeing, because the sky was cloudy.

Having thought in mind for a few minutes about her wealthy mother, she simpered at herself and then said loudly "Hoh! this is the end of my life and I am already in my grave while I am still alive! Hah! when I was with my wealthy mother, she never failed to provide me my breakfast or lunch or refreshment. But I have not tasted even a drop of water now over three days! If I were not a silly person I should have obeyed my mother's and other persons' warning—not to attempt to know the 'punishment' and the 'poverty'. But I am now in the great punishment and in gravy poverty as well! A few hours later, Rali and I were lost ourselves and I have nobody here now with whom to be discussing! Yesterday, I fought the Satyr of the Dark Jungle and I conquered him!

"Today, the eagle took me from the rock and it threw me into this hole!

"Of course, perhaps if Rali could find out the way and go back to our village, she would tell my mother that I have taken away by an eagle!

"And it is this day I believe the old people's saying—one who has done what one has never done, shall see what one has never seen!"

After Simbi had discussed like that within herself with embarrassment, she felt to eat. "Hah! what can I eat now?" after she asked herself painfully, then she sat up

right, she paused for a while. And then she cut a soft part
of the tree, she looked at it for a few seconds and then
threw it into the mouth. She chewed it for many minutes
but at last she vomited it having failed to swallow it.
Then more than one gallon of tears rolled down her
chicks within that moment.

And she stood up unexpectedly, she walked round the
hole. She knocked it heavily and cried loudly, perhaps
someone would hear all that noises and come to help her
out. But there was nobody who was near, even the sound
of the knocks and her shouts did not travel to the outside
of the tree.

Then she came back and sat on her mattress. She put
one of her fingers in the mouth, she held it with teeth so
mercilessly that it nearly to cut and then she uttered with
great sorrow "Hah! hah! hah! my mother . . ."

But before she could utter the whole of what she had
wanted to say, about four fruits fell onto her right
shoulder by mistake from the eaglets. And she was greatly
feared for she thought they were harmful things. But
when she took them from the shoulder and discovered
them fruits, she started to eat them at once.

When it was five days that she was inside the hole, she
became mad for thinking of her great mistake which she
had made for leaving her wealthy mother.

Many dead goats, fowls, etc. which were bringing to
the eaglets by their mothers were falling from them into
the hole by mistake. But she had no fire with which to
roast them and eat them. She was simply looking at these
dead animals.

Simbi became the wife of the Woodcutter

One day, a half dead big boa fell into the hole by mistake from those eaglets. And Simbi was shrank up with fear when she saw it.

After some minutes, the boa became completely alive and then it began to glide round her.

Having done that for a few minutes, it raised itself up from the ground. It opened its mouth in such a fearful way and it was gliding slowly towards her just to swallow her.

But at that moment she had lost all her senses and then she started to stagger round the hole just to safe herself and the boa was chasing her about to be swallowed.

Having done that for some time, luckily, it discovered those dead animals. Then it stopped there and swallowed some of them so greedily that it could not move about but lay down helplessly before the rest (dead animals).

This boa was so fearful to Simbi that she started to strike her head heavily to every part of the hole just to kill herself at once. Because she believed that however it might be she would die there. Therefore she did not want to suffer for a long time. Of course, she was feeding from all the fruits which were falling into the hole from the eaglets etc.

"I have now satisfied my hunger with some of these fruits. But what can I do now next? Oh yes, I remember, I have been a good singer in those days that I was in happiness and with my mother! I do better sing a song now! But what kind of a song is suitable for this my melancholy?

"Yes! yes! yes! I remember, I had once gone with my

mother to a house in which an old man died, and on that
day, I sang the song of mourn with those whom we met
there!

"I shall sing that song here now, because I believe in a
few days' time, I shall die!"

Then Simbi sang that song for a few minutes before
she fell asleep unnoticed, because she had never slept for
a moment since when she was thrown inside the hole.

And she woke in the dawn by the hisses of that boa. It
had already coiled round her before she woke. But when
she opened her eyes, she met the mouth of that boa wide
open and was nearly to touch her own head.

Having seen this again, she was shouting for help.
After a while, her throat stuck together for long shouting,
and then she was feeling to drink water badly.

But as she was pretending to kill herself at once, she
noticed that the hole became entirely dark, and a few
seconds after, a heavy rain came. And immediately the
rain started, the thunder was roaring from the sky into
the hole. It was sounding so heavily inside the hole that
it nearly to blow up the hole and that boa was so feared
the sounding that it ran to the corner of the hole and hid
itself there.

"What has happened again?" Simbi whispered as if
she would die if she spoke aloud. After a while, a lightning flashed from the sky into the hole. And at the same
moment it started to burn the refuses very slowly. Having
seen this, Simbi ran to it, she managed it until it became
a big fire.

After she had warmed her body from it, she remem-

bered to roast some of that dead animals and she roasted
a fowl and ate some of it, because she was unable to finish
the whole of it.

Hardly stopped to eat the roasted fowl when she
noticed that a part of the tree had caught the fire. And a
few seconds later, the whole of that hole caught the fire.
Then she was running to every part of the hole just to
escape the fire.

She was so puzzled at that moment that she attempted
to fly out of the hole. She flapped both arms perhaps she
would be able to fly like a bird, but all her efforts were
failed, for she had no wings. "Ho!-o! ha!-a! hu!-u! My
mother! my dead father appear here now and take me
out! yay! yay!" thus she shouted in vain.

Having turned round the hole for some minutes the
hairs of her head and her clothes caught the fire as well.
"I shall faint! I shall faint! I shall fain . . . t." Then with
embarrassment she fell down and fainted.

But as she was doing all this, the fire had turned into a
big flame and it had appeared to the sky from the top of
the tree. The thick smoke was rushing to such a great
height in the sky that it was easily seeing from a long
distance.

The smoke and the flame drove away all the eagles,
parrots, hawks, etc. who were living on top of the tree.
They scattered in the sky and were flying round the top
of the tree and were trying to take their young ones away
from the smoke, but they were unable to do it.

After a while a woodcutter saw this smoke and the
flame from a long distance.

Simbi became the wife of the Woodcutter

"Look at the smoke and flame coming out from a tree!" the woodcutter told his son who was about twelve years of age.

"Yes, I see it, but I am afraid, something must have happened in that area!" the son raised his head up and explained. "Perhaps a bush is burning near there!" the father (woodcutter) suggested. "If it is so or not let us go there perhaps we shall be able to kill some of the birds," advised the son.

Then the woodcutter and his son were coming there with their cutting instruments as hastily as their feet could lift them up.

After a few minutes they came to the tree and they were greatly wondered when they saw the numerous birds which were flying round the top of the tree.

"It is better to cut down this tree at once, because I believe there must be something strange inside its hole," the father told his son. But the son was unable to answer, because the noises of the birds and the hisses of the flame were downed his voice.

"Bring! bring the instruments here and let us cut it down at once!" he waved hands to his son.

When the instruments were brought, the father started to cut one part and the son was cutting it at the other part with axes. A few minutes later, they cut the tree to its hole. "Let us cut it wider so that we may see every part of the hole," he told his son. But immediately they cut it to the hole and when the fresh air rushed in Simbi had become half conscious, before they had cut it to such a large size that they wanted it to be.

Having cut it to the size that they wanted it to be, he and his son peeped through the wide space with the intention to kill the animals which probably might be inside that hole.

"Hah! what is this?" both feared and exclaimed the same words at a time and with great fear they jerked their heads back at once.

"Is that a human or a nymph?" the son wondered. "Of course, I cannot say the real creature it is, at this moment!" the father was surprised so much that he did not know what to say at that moment.

"All right, let us peep into the hole again just to make sure of the right kind of the creature it is." Then he and his son peeped in again. But yet they could not hesitate and look well for what they had seen for the first time. And only Simbi's head they could see in the darkness.

"Hah! this is the human's head!" both jerked their heads back and stood up right on the alert. They looked at each other's eyes with astonishment and fear and then paused for a while.

"It is possible for a human to be in this hole?" the son asked his father. But the father was so much embarrassed that he was unable to reply. But when they stoned at the head, then Simbi said with a very weak voice "I am a human being and not a nymph. I am thrown inside the hole by an eagle. Please safe me out." And then their fear dispelled immediately Simbi explained herself to them.

Then they advised her to stretch out her arms through the space which they had cut. And she crept near to the space and then stretched her arms to them.

Simbi became the wife of the Woodcutter

In the first instance they thought that it was an easy job to pull Simbi out. Then the father pulled her, he thought he alone could do it. But he failed entirely having tried all his power.

"All right, let both of us join hands together and pull her right out," he told his son. Then with both hands he held Simbi's right hand and his son held her left hand with both hands, and then pulled her. But still they were not strong enough to pull her out.

"Let us try more," the son said after they had rested for a few minutes. And they pulled her with all their power, but yet they were unable to pull her out.

Not knowing that as they were trying to pull her out by force, it was so that boa which was inside the hole, was swallowing Simbi's legs and then it was pulling her back to the hole, of course Simbi did not feel that the boa was swallowing her legs because both (legs) had already cramped.

After the father and his son had rested for the second time, they held her hands as usual and then the father commanded "One! two! three ee!" Willing or not, they pulled Simbi out together with the boa by force. Although they threw her hands down and run to a short distance just to safe their lives from the boa immediately they saw it that it had already swallowed half of her body.

After some minutes they came back. With great care they killed that boa and then pulled Simbi out of its mouth.

But before they had finished all of that, Simbi had fainted again for rough pulling.

"Hah! this lady is too fine and beautiful than to leave her in this place until she shall be suffered to death. It is better to take her to the town for the treatment!" the father or woodcutter exclaimed immediately they dragged Simbi to the outside of the hole.

"Yes, that is better," the son replied.

"But with what can we take her to the town because I am afraid, she is now delicate to handle for her appearance is scraggy?" the son feared, because he was too young to understand as how to handle such a weary and helpless person as this one.

"Thank you my son. It is very simple to take her to the town, and I will show you today the right way a helpless person as this one is taking to the town or to a safe place."

Having explained like that to his son, he cut some slender sticks and some strong ropes. He cut all the sticks a little above the height of Simbi. With the ropes and the sticks he formed them into a frame work and that was a stretcher.

After that he cut plenty of leaves, he spread them on the stretcher in such a way that the sticks would not hurt Simbi. Having done that, he and his son put her on it very gently. And then they covered her feet to the neck with broad leaves, because all her clothes had burnt away by the fire when she was inside the hole.

After, he tied a strong long rope to the head of that boa which they had already killed. He gave the second end of the rope to his son to hold it. Then he hung all their cutting instruments on his shoulder. After that he and his son put the stretcher on heads. The father carried it at the front while the son carried it at back. And they were carrying her to the town and the son was towing the boa with the rope towards his back, they were going to eat it.

Simbi became the wife of the Woodcutter

Having travelled for two hours, they reached their town. And immediately they put her in the room. The woodcutter and his son started to beat the broken pot and calabash near her head, so that the soundings might call her spirit back to her from heaven's road. Having beaten the broken pot, etc. for a few minutes, her spirit returned to her, she started to feel as a person might feel. At that time she could swallow all the medicines which were giving to her, and all the necroses of the boa bites were treated with another kind of a medicine.

Thus Simbi was saved out of the hole by the woodcutter.

"Rali! Rali! Rali!" that was the first word which Simbi exclaimed since when she had brought from the hole to the town. She thought that she was still with Rali who was still wandering about in the Dark Jungle.

She never knew where she was and never knew who had saved her. All was just a dream to her.

"Who is Rali?" the woodcutter asked softly. "I think I am with Rali now. Rali is a lady with whom I had been travelling before I had been taken away by the eagle. Please can you know whereabouts she is at present?" Simbi explained and asked after she had become conscious. "I don't know who is Rali and I don't know whereabouts she is."

Within a few weeks Simbi's condition was so improved that it seemed as if she had not met any difficulty since when she was born.

"Many thanks, the woodcutter. But I am sorry that I have no money to pay for you for the treatments you have given me before I recovered and for the wonderful work you have done before you saved me out of the hole. But, be sure that God will pay another thing for you which will be even better than my 'thanks'.

"And this is to tell you that I am continuing my journey tomorrow morning, and I shall be grateful if you will be good enough to show me a safe path from this town to my village."

"Where is your village?" the woodcutter wondered. "My village is far away from here," Then the wood-cutter explained that there was no another path after the Path of Death. "Is that so?" Simbi asked calmly. "It is so, Simbi. But I wonder, what had forced you to leave your village?" he asked when he thought over of all the punishments, etc. which she had met before he had saved her and he thought as well of uncountable punish-ments, etc. which she was still going to meet ahead, probably before she would die.

"You see, Mr. Woodcutter, it was after I had been kid-napped from my village by a man called Dogo, I found out that I had made a mistake to tell my wealthy mother that I liked to know the punishment and the poverty. She warned me not to attempt to do that, but I disobeyed her. And since from when Dogo had kidnapped me and sold me from hand to hand, I was struggling hardly to go back to my mother but all were in vain."

"Will you let me marry you? If you do agree, I promise, that a few months after the marriage, I shall take you back to your village," the woodcutter deceived her in respect of her beauty. Because she was so beautiful

94

at that time that a crowd of people used to come to the woodcutter's house just to enjoy her beauty for a few minutes. And whenever she was going to somewhere in that town, several people would be rushing here and there just to look at her beauty.

"I am afraid, Mr. Woodcutter, you are trying now just to obstruct my leaving. But all your activities before you saved me implied that whatever a promise you give to a person you will fulfil it.

"And in respect of that, I do agree to your request. But I bring it to your notice now that in the future, if you fail to take me back to my village, the 'day will be changed into the night' for you."

Now Simbi had turned to the wife of the woodcutter. Unfortunately, after some months Simbi delivered of a male baby. And within a few months the baby developed to such a state that Simbi could not depart from it for a moment. And she was in happiness every day in respect of her baby. Although when several people used to die in one day in this town, and as this had never happened or it was an unusual bad omen for the king, the king asked from his god the kind of the sacrifice which was to be made to expel the unusual death from the town.

The god explained that before the death could be expelled a living baby would be put in a wooden mortar and plenty of soap would be put as well. After that the mother of that baby would pound the baby together with the soap thoroughly. After that the soap would be distributed among the people of the town. And having washed their bodies with that juju-soap for three times, the death would not be able to approach anybody to be killed having smelt the smell of the juju-soap from that person's body, the god said.

But as there was none of the natives of this town who could volunteer her baby, therefore Simbi's baby was taken from her by force, being she was not a native, and they forced her to pound the baby with the soap.

She wept bitterly when she was pounding her baby, but all was in vain. Having seen this bad habit, she was feeling to go away from this town, until she delivered another baby. But it was at that time the people of this town heard the information that the locusts were coming to their farms. And Simbi's baby was among the sacrifices which they prepared and put at the junction of paths just to drive the locusts to another place, and it was so when they did it.

Now, Simbi was in a great sadness. She told the wood-cutter, her husband, to take her to her village, but he was telling her to wait for some weeks. But when she discovered that it was a lie and he did not know where her village was, then she repeated her curse and at the same moment, the woodcutter's day changed into the night. He could not see anything and it was in the darkness he was when Simbi continued her journey from that town. But after a few days that she had left him, his day changed to as usual, he could see. For he had done good to Simbi, otherwise he would remain in the darkness throughout his life time. Then he chased her to bring her back to his house and be his wife as usual. But all his efforts were failed. Simbi had gone far away.

CHAPTER NINE

For me and for my Gods

Simbi was travelling on and on until she came to a land and that was the land of poverty. Although she was in sadness at being away from the town of the woodcutter.

This land of poverty was too wonderful because all the clothes of her body turned into ashes immediately she started to travel on it. She was then in nakedness.

Having travelled for many hours she was ambitious to eat. Then she went to a tree to pluck some fruits and eat them. But to her great horror, immediately she touched the fruits just to pluck them, they turned into small stones. She was unable to eat them. Then she left there. A few minutes later, she travelled to a pond of water. As she was hungry badly for food she thought to drink some water perhaps she would be more powerful. But when she bent down just to start to drink that water it dried at once.

But at last when she noticed that it was the land of poverty she was travelling along as hastily as possible just to leave there in time.

Having left that land, she came to a path and she could not distinguish this path from the Path of Death. But

97

anyhow she was travelling along on it until she came to a stream of water.

She stopped there and drank some water, though there was no food at all. But as she needed the looking glass and there was none, she sat down closely to this stream. She bent her head downward onto the water. And her shadow proved that she had leaned, the hairs of her head had become almost dust for want of care and she was greatly ashamed to see herself in nakedness. All these things had happened to her immediately she had entered the land of poverty.

With shame she left the stream at once. After a while she travelled to a bush. She cut plenty of broad leaves. She stitched them together with ropes. She wrapped her body with it as if it was a cloth. Having done that, she began to travel along on that path until she came to a house. The house was near this path.

As she was feeling to eat from a long time, she entered the house. She met an old woman inside it. She sat in a corner. She noticed that the house was full of all kinds of gods, who were the neighbours of the old woman. Because there was no any human being there with her. She was the owner of those gods. Although several food sellers and drapers were visiting there occasionally just to sell their merchandise. And she was buying clothes and food from them for herself and for her gods.

"Good afternoon here," Simbi knocked the door and saluted with faint voice, for she was nearly to die of hunger by that time.

"Good afternoon, for whose voice shows that of a

lady," the old woman answered quietly from her usual sitting corner. And she was so old that she could only distinguish the voice of a man or a woman.

Then Simbi entered and with sharp sight she discovered the old woman sat down in a dark corner, although she was about to run out with fear when she perceived those gods which nearly occupied the whole house.

"Can I thank for something to eat?" she knelt before the old woman and asked softly.

"Oh! I am sorry, the bananas which you are looking before me now, are for me and for my gods only," the woman replied.

"What about the food which is near you?" "And that food is for me and for my gods as well," she explained.

"All right, can I thank for the water to drink then?" "What? the water is for me and for my gods," she replied sharply.

"I think, you see me now that I am so poor that I can only wear leaves as a cloth?" Simbi said. "Yes I see you." the old woman replied after she had tried and opened her dim eyes. "All right, can I thank for a cover cloth which is hung before your gods?" "Hah! not at all, that cloth cannot be spared because it is for me and for my gods and the rest things that I have are for me and for my gods only!" she replied without being sorry for Simbi.

"Hah! what kind of an old woman is this? Everything you ask from her, she will reply, 'is for me and for my gods'.

"Madam! can I pawn myself to you then so that I can buy some clothes with the money you give me and to be spending the rest money for buying my food while I am working for you?" Simbi asked for a loan because she could not leave this old woman and continue her journey without food and clothes on her body.

"Of course, I am not a pawn broker, but if you will be faithful to me and to my gods, I will lend you some amount of money with which you will buy some clothes to be wearing instead of the leaves which are now on your body. And you will be spending the rest money for buying your food."

"Yes, madam, I shall be faithful to you and to your gods," Simbi promised. "You are not going to make a promise simply like that, but you will swear before me and my gods, that you will be faithful to me and that you will not betray my gods," the old woman bursted into a great laughter when Simbi simply promised before her and not before her gods as well.

Then Simbi knelt down before the gods and the old woman cut a part of her left thumb with a knife, and the blood which came out of the cut was dropped onto the gods.

"I shall not betray you," Simbi swore before the gods. After that the money was loaned to her. Thus Simbi became a maid of this old woman.

The second day that she had given her the loan, the cloth seller and food seller came there. And with a part of the money she bought some clothes and she was spending the rest for buying food.

For me and for my Gods

"Have you sacrificed to the gods?" "Have you drawn water to the house?" "Have you washed the clothes for the week end?" "Have you cooked my food?" "Yes, madam." Thus the old woman used to ask from Simbi every day.

But when she believed that Simbi was faithful to her gods and to herself and in everything without giving her anything to eat, she gave her some of the gods as prizes and she taught her how to be worshipping them and how to be asking helps from each of them.

These three gods were the god of thunder, the god of famine and the god of iron respectively.

She warned Simbi to be taking great care of them for they would be her saviour in future. After that, she gave her a satchel in which she kept them.

"These three gods are the prizes of your faith," the old woman said.

CHAPTER TEN

Simbi back to the Dark Jungle

But after some weeks since when Simbi had inherited the three gods—

One midnight, the Satyr of the Dark Jungle with whom she had fought the other day, heard the information that Simbi was living with that old woman. And as he was still looking about for her so that he might revenge from her of what she had done to him when both fought, came to the old woman's house after Simbi and the old woman had slept.

He woke Simbi alone, he explained that he came to take her back to the Dark Jungle where he would kill her. Simbi was so puzzled that she did not know what to do immediately heard like that from him. But instead to wake the old woman and tell her to assist her to help her fight this Satyr, she ran to the corner that she put the satchel in which her three gods were put. She hung it on her left shoulder and then she took one cutlass. After that she came back to him and started to fight him with the intention that her gods would help her to conquer him.

But the Satyr slapped at her breast instead to fight her in return. And she became to the size of a baby. Without hesitation, he vomited a big bottle, he put her inside it by force, and before the old woman woke he had taken her to the Dark Jungle.

Then he put that bottle on a rock, after that he invited some evil creatures of his kind. All of them sat round the rock, and they were looking at Simbi inside the bottle as they were drinking a certain drink. The Satyr told them that he was going to kill Simbi in a few days' time. But Simbi feared greatly when she heard like that.

"What can I do now which can safe me out of this bottle?" She was confused entirely.

A few minutes later, she remembered to ask for a help from her gods. "Please, the god of thunder, help me to come out from this bottle." She hardly said like that when the god of thunder sent the lightning onto that rock suddenly. It broke the rock and the bottle into several pieces and the Satyr with his invitees ran far away with fear. Without hesitation Simbi left there for another part of the Dark Jungle before the Satyr came back.

It was at that time Simbi believed that her gods could help her and then she held them as her soldiers.

Then she was wandering about in that jungle. A few days later she met Rali, Sala, Kadara, the rest nameless refugees and Bako, under a tree. They sat and were thinking seriously of the way to come out of this Dark Jungle, and they were thinking as well as how they could escape from Bako, the cockish lady. Because she was giving them much troubles.

But as Simbi was explaining to them with a dead voice all her difficulties, the phoenix who was the helper of the

Satyr, suspected that they hid under that tree. And it pounced on them and took one of the nameless refugees away unexpectedly.

Then the rest left that place for another one.

SIMBI AND THE PHOENIX, THE SATYR'S ASSISTANCE

A few minutes after that the phoenix had carried one of them away, it came again and started to jump from one branch to another, it was looking for them.

And immediately they had seen it, they were hiding themselves in the darkness. If it took one direction they would take another direction, and by so doing it was unable to find them out, but it did not go away.

After a while, to make sure the right place that they hid, this phoenix screeched horribly.

But Bako, the cockish lady, who was among them, started to crow continuously immediately she heard the horrible cry of the phoenix.

"Please, Bako, stop crowing, it would suspect us to the phoenix," the rest warned her whisperly.

"Heigh! don't tell me that or don't you know I ought to be acting here as my Siamese twin sister is acting at home!" Bako explained to them so loudly that the phoenix heard and then it was coming to them. Having seen them, it dashed to them just to take one of them away.

But it was unable to do it, when Simbi started to cut every part of its body with the cutlass which she took with her from that old woman's house, when the Satyr went there and put her inside the bottle.

Simbi back to the Dark Jungle

Within a few minutes, the phoenix flew away when it could not bear the cuts any longer. When it believed that it could not hesitate and take some of them away, for the fear of the cutlass with which Simbi was cutting its body, then it flew high in the sky with a very large stone, and it screeched suddenly just to make sure the right spot that they hid and then to throw that stone on them.

Unfortunately Bako started to crow loudly immediately she heard its horrible screech and this showed it where they were. And then it released the stone. The stone pressed many of them to death. Then the rest rushed to another spot and hid there. They tried to drive Bako back from them but she did not agree, she was shouting greatly instead.

It was like that the phoenix was throwing heavy stones on them until it killed Kadara, Sala and all the nameless refugees, and it remained Simbi, Rali and Bako, the cockish lady, who was suspecting them out to the phoenix.

The Satyr was greatly admired the work of the phoenix. Although he himself was struggling about in the jungle to find them out and kill all of them at once, but he never saw them.

When it was in the mid night, Simbi was feeling cold so much that if she did not warm herself with fire, doubtless she would die before the day-break, of course the rest were feeling the cold but not as much as she did.

As she was discussing about the cold with the rest, she remembered her three gods. Then she commanded the god of thunder to provide the fire.

Hardly commanded it, when it sent the fire onto a dead

wood which was near them. The dead wood had a hole which was an impasse.

Within thirty minutes, it had burnt the hole very far and it shone to a very long distance. Then Simbi with the rest were warming their bodies from it. But as Bako did not stop of crowing because she was enjoying the warmth giving to her by the fire, when the phoenix was hearing her crow, it discovered the fire and it was quite sure that they were before it. Instead to throw stone on them as usual, it dashed from the sky to them, but it could only carry Bako away. Having seen this, Simbi and Rali left there for another spot, they hid there.

After a while the phoenix came again, and as it was still seeing the fire from the sky it thought that the rest were still there and it dashed towards the fire, but it flew inside the hole of the tree by a mistake.

It struggled hardly to come out but it was in vain, the fire burnt it into ashes at the same time.

It was like that the phoenix, the Satyr's assistance, was killed.

Before the day-break, news had reached the satyr and the whole evil creatures of this Dark Jungle, that a number of refugees had killed the phoenix.

CHAPTER ELEVEN

Simbi and the Satyr of the Dark Jungle

As the death of the phoenix was a great loss to the whole creatures of the Dark Jungle, particularly to the Satyr, therefore every one of them joined the Satyr who was their guard, to fight Simbi to death at all costs.

Then they scattered into the jungle, everyone with fighting weapons and the Satyr himself held his cudgel of bone. A few days after, they traced Simbi and Rali out. Then they surrounded them at once, with the intention to capture them alive and after that to suffer them to death.

Having seen them that they had already surrounded her and Rali, she believed, however she might be powerful, they would capture her. So, she put the satchel of her gods down. Without hesitation, she loosened it and then took out all the three gods.

Then she asked from them to help her fight all the evil creatures. Hardly asked for the help when a heavy rain came. As it was raining heavily it was so the god of thunder was sending the powerful lightning onto these creatures continuously and it was killing a large number of them each time that it roared.

107

But as the rest were still approaching nearer instead to go away, the god of famine sent incalculable locusts to them. Within a few minutes, the locusts had eaten all their crops which they were eating. Having eaten the whole crops, they started to eat these creatures themselves. Within one hour that the rain started a big river was formed, and it carried them back to where they were coming from while the locusts covered almost their bodies and the lightning was dropping on them continuously.

After the lightning and the rain were stopped, then the locusts flew away. Having freed from all these troubles they gave up to fight Simbi and everyone went back to his house.

But this noxious Satyr did not satisfy to give up except to fight Simbi to death. And Simbi left that spot and started to find the right path on which to travel to her village at the same. She looked for Rali, but she had escaped to another part of the jungle immediately the fight had started. For she thought those evil creatures would kill Simbi and herself.

For two days, the Satyr did not approach Simbi at all. But he was thinking of the way he would kill her instead.

"Oh yes, I remember, the fearful lady [Simbi] told me when she conquered me the other day, that she was a singer. Therefore I will build a wonderful hall and I will put many creatures there to be singing there every day and night. And I believe, the lady will enter the hall to sing with those creatures, and then I will be able to capture her from the hall!" The Satyr remembered that

Simbi and the Satyr of the Dark Jungle

Simbi had told him the day that she conquered him, before she was thrown into the hole of a tree, she was a singer and that her song could kill and wake a person.

SIMBI WAS CAUGHT AND PUNISHED BY THE SATYR

Then the Satyr went to a part of the Dark Jungle. He vomited one magic, he put it on the ground, then he commanded it to become a beautiful hall and it was so at the same moment. Having done all that, he hid himself near the hall with the intention that Simbi would discover the hall whenever she travelled to that area and doubtless she would enter it to sing.

This hall was about forty feet square. All the walls were living migratory birds, the windows and roof were another kind of a singing birds. The plumages of all the birds were made of pure gold, their feet and beaks were white.

But when Simbi had failed to find out the right path of her village, she stopped, and rested. After some days, she discovered a huge hole which contained her to sleep. Then she was living inside it.

One day, when she had nothing to eat, she left her gods inside the hole, and then she was wandering about in search for the edible fruits to eat.

After a while, she travelled to some pawpaw trees. She plucked two pawpaws. Hardly ate all when she noticed that all the living creatures were running helter-skelter. And within that moment a heavy wind started. The wind was so blowing with its full power that the topmosts of small and big trees were touching the ground and then getting up at once. All the refuses as leaves, dried sticks and dusts were full up in the sky, everything was in disorder.

At that critical time Simbi could not go back to her hole and she was so perplexed that she did not remember the time she started from that spot to find about where she could shelter herself. It was from that spot she started to experience the punishment and poverty of the Dark Jungle, because immediately she started to find the shelter a heavy rain came. She was so drenched by the rain that all her clothes were stuck to her body and a few minutes after, they tore into rags, but she was still going on with them because she could not remain in this heavy rain or in the powerful wind.

After a while she travelled to that hall which was a bait for her. Then she stopped and was listening to those birds which were singing a kind of a melodious song that which she had never heard since when she was born, though she was a good singer as well.

Having enjoyed the song for a while she entered the hall. Of course, if it was not for that song, she would fear greatly to enter it, especially as it was formed with migratory birds, etc.

Having entered, she saw a band of orchestra in the corner of this hall. They were busy with their instruments at that moment.

Those who were playing the instruments to the song of the birds, were just in form of shadows of angels, and they were seemed as if they were touched with hand perhaps the hand would not hold or feel anything. All were dressed in the multi-coloured clothes which had several ornaments that the hand could not make.

To Simbi's greatest fear and astonishment was that sometimes, only the faces of these orchestras would be visible to her and the rest parts of their bodies would lose to her view, and a few minutes after their bodies would be visible and their faces would be lost to her view, and sometimes only their hands would be visible, they (hands) would be playing on the instruments and several melodious songs would be singing with the only visible mouths.

After a few minutes, they were visible to her completely. And as she was a singer, so at the same moment a kind of a song came to her mind, and immediately she opened her mouth and started to sing it to their instruments. To her greatest surprise, it was this very song the whole of them started to sing and she was singing it with them and they were playing also their instruments to it, which conformed with the song at the same time.

Immediately they joined her to sing the song, she lost all her senses, because the tone with which they were singing it was so melodious that she started to dance from the long distance that she stood until she reached the place that all of them sat down on the specially arranged seats, and she sat down before them. But she was still dancing in a slow motion to her left and right, and to her back and front, according to how the instruments were playing. It was so she was looking at everyone of them with surprise, because she had never acrossed such a wonderful orchestra as that one.

Having looked at them for some minutes, then they changed their tones to another lovely tones unexpectedly. But as she was more interested in this than the first one, she stood up suddenly with great joy and then started to dance to every part of the hall as if she was a mad lady.

When she danced back to them, she bowed down before them showing them the great admiration she had in the way of their singing and playing of the instruments. But it was a great pity that Simbi never aware that the Satyr hid near there and he was looking at her as she was doing all these things, and she did not know that the hall was a trap which the Satyr set for her.

But as she bowed down before them, it came to her mind at that moment that these creatures who were playing the instruments and singing her song with her, were not human beings in anyway, because the way of their singing and playing the instruments were beyond the human power. Then she feared to remain in that hall with them. But at the same moment that they noticed she was leaving the hall, plenty of the ultra-beautiful ladies rushed out of the room that the birds formed within that moment in a corner of the hall, they surrounded her and were dancing with her at the same moment.

They were dressed in snow white attires which were full of the superfine decorations. The hairs on their heads were glossy and were adorned with the decorations of gold flower, etc. which were glistening in the darkness. Everyone of them wore silver bead on neck, but Simbi was unable to describe the kind of the metal which they wore on their wrists, for all their snow white attires were sewn in long sleeves. All of them were neat and smart.

A few minutes later, those who were singing and playing the instruments all the while, changed that song to another one and the instruments were then giving out a very steadily soundings.

When Simbi was hearing this music she lost all her senses and forgot that she had met several difficulties and that she was going to meet more. And then she started to dance with those ultra-beautiful ladies, although none of them talked to her and she did not talk to them as well.

Having danced with them for a while, she raised her head up. But when she noticed that all the birds which were formed the hall were singing as well, she was greatly feared at that time, and she believed that all of those creatures with whom she was dancing and singing were not human. Then she ran to her left just to break the circle and go out of the hall. But the beautiful ladies danced to that direction and they disturbed her to go out. And she danced to the right and they did the same thing, they were keeping her back to the circle so that she might not be able to go out of the hall.

When Simbi understood that they did not want her to go away, she wanted to break the circle by force, and the ladies were not strong enough to keep her in by that moment. But as they were still rushing here and there in the hall in trying to prevent her from not going out, six big fearful ostriches rushed out of the same room from which those ladies had come out. White shoes were on their hoofs and their faces were covered with white masks.

Immediately they came to them, the ladies parted for them to pass in to the circle and they (ostriches) surrounded Simbi so that she might not get chance to run away.

Having done that, the ladies disappeared at once. Then those ostriches started to chase her and were pretending to swallow her, and she was turning round the circle just to safe herself from them.

At last, when their attitudes were too fearful to her, she feared greatly. She fell down unexpectedly and it was like that she fell asleep unnoticed. But it was a great pity to Simbi after all, that those creatures were just illuding her so that she might not be felt to leave the hall until the Satyr would come there and then take her away.

And she enjoyed the sleep for two hours. But when she was just dreaming and was seeing in her dream that Kadara, Sala, Bako and the nameless refugees who had been taken away by the phoenix, were in severe punishments, which made her body to be shocking at that moment for the fear that probably in the near future she too would be punished like that by the Satyr—

There entered the hall, the Satyr, and he came to her, although she never wake at the time he entered and she did not know the time that those ostriches disappeared.

Then the Satyr slapped her so suddenly that she woke and stood up unexpectedly. She looked for those orchestra and those ostriches but all of them had gone away and she was very sad at the same time when she did not hear anybody singing in the hall as before she had fallen asleep. Of course, all the birds which were the wall, etc. were still singing. But she was greatly terrified when she turned her head back and saw the Satyr behind her. He scrowled and started to tell her with horrible voice—"This is the Satyr before you now! My trap has caught you and you are going now to where you shall be punished to death! Have you any power now? can you safe yourself from me now? Not at all! You have turned into my food! Hah a a! You hopeless lady who have nearly ruined the whole of my people! By the way, where are the rest of you? Of course, as I catch you thus I shall catch the rest of you! Don't you know that this hall is a bait for you?" Thus the Satyr roared horribly on Simbi. But she was unable to reply him. She simply stood before him as if she was dead, because she had left all her three gods which were her power, inside the hole in which she was living before she discovered the hall.

The Satyr hardly roared on her when he put her on head. After that he cried so loudly and terribly that the whole of this Dark Jungle shook to left and right for some minutes, and that was the sign he made to his people that Simbi, their enemy, was already caught. But immediately he shouted like that, all the birds which were the wall, roof, etc., for the hall flew away and there was nothing remained at the site of the hall.

Then he was carrying Simbi along in this Dark Jungle. After a while he came to a big rock and he climbed it to the top.

Hardly climbed the rock to the top when his people

hurtled there when they heard his cry. Then he and with some of them lay Simbi flatly on that rock by force. After that both her arms were parted to left and right being she faced the sky, and then both feet were straightened. Having done all this, the Satyr provoked a kind of a charm onto her body. And both feet to half part of her body changed into the part of that rock at the same moment, and both her arms were changed from her shoulders downward into the part of the rock as well. After that, the Satyr started to beat her with his cudgel of bone. Simbi was crying with her topmost voice but none of them listened to her. She struggled hardly to stand up and run away but all her efforts were failed, because her feet and arms had already changed into the rock.

When the Satyr stopped to beat her, all the rest of his people were beating her greedily with anything they could find thereabout. Having done that for a few minutes, they scorned her and then the whole of them went back to their dwelling places with the satisfaction of minds that they had caught one who had been punished them.

Very early in the morning, the Satyr went there with his usual cudgel of bone. He beat Simbi for one hour before he went away.

Immediately he went away, another evil spirit came with hot water, he threw it on Simbi, after that he flogged her for a few minutes and then he left there. "Can I free from these punishment?" Simbi asked from her heart seriously. "Certainly, you will free from it," her heart replied quietly. "How long that will be?" she asked sorrowfully.

"In the near future."

"I don't believe so," she asked.

"You must believe," her heart assured her.

"All right, if it will be so, by whom?"

"By one whom you have saved his life," her heart replied sharply.

Thus she was discussing with her heart, when about one thousand of these evil creatures together with the Satyr, the noxious creature, came. Then they started to beat her and they beat her till the evening before they left there. Simbi wept bitterly till she had no power to shake her body or to make any sign of pain whenever they were beating her. She suffered greatly for food, water, cold and for the heat of the sun but these evil creatures had no mercy on her.

One night, the rain came, it was so heavy that within two hours from when it started the water absolutely covered her body. Luckily when the water was about to swallow the whole of her body together with that rock, it became a powerful stream of water. And at the same time it was pushing the rock along to another part of this Dark Jungle.

When it pushed it to a short distance from the Satyr's dwelling place, then it was stopped by a big tree. The surroundings of the Satyr's dwelling place or house was too terrible to see or to remain there for some minutes. When Simbi saw it, she was nearly to faint for fear, especially when she remembered all kinds

117

of the punishments which were going to give her in the morning.

As she was thinking all of that in mind, there appeared the very gnome who had saved her when she was tied to the tree to be killed in the town of the multi-coloured people, the town in which Bako became a cock when she stole the old woman's hen. The gnome stood before her and said "I have been hearing you crying sorrowfully from a long distance. What are you crying so loudly and sorrowfully for?"

"Look at both my feet to the thighs and then look at both my hands to the shoulders how all have changed into the rock," Simbi said whisperly.

"Hah! who has done this?" the gnome was greatly excited when he saw that both her feet and arms were petrified.

"Eh, talk softly so that the Satyr may not wake, look at his house near here. Let me explain to you, I had once fought and conquered the Satyr before I had been thrown into the hole of a tree by an eagle. And again when I came back to this Dark Jungle, the Satyr with the rest evil creatures and the phoenix started to fight me and the other refugees just to revenge of what I had done to the Satyr from me and from the rest refugees.

"But with the help of my three gods, I killed the phoenix and several of the rest evil creatures were wounded. Although the phoenix had carried away Sala, Kadara, Bako and the rest refugees before it was killed.

"After he had struggled to kill me but failed, then he built an illusive hall, the wall, roof, etc. were migratory

118

birds. And I entered the hall in respect of its beauty and the melodious songs which I heard from there. Having danced and sung for a few hours with the creatures that I met there, I feared greatly and I felt to leave there. But as those creatures were still deceiving me with the dance and songs, I fell asleep unnoticed. And then the Satyr came in there, he woke me up and he carried me from there and put me on this rock. He changed my feet and arms into the rock as you see them. And since from that day, the Satyr and the rest creatures are coming to me every morning and evening, they are punishing me nearly to death before they would leave me and go away," Simbi explained painfully to the gnome.

"Is that so?" the gnome wondered. "Yes it is so, even if you can hide near here till the morning, you will see them when they will come to punish me," Simbi said calmly.

"What kind of a help do you want from me?" the gnome asked. "I shall be happy if you will change me now back to my usual form and after that I want you to show me the right path to my village, so that I may go back at the same time, because I have fed up with all the punishments and poverties which I used to meet every day and night, every hour and minute since from when I had been kidnapped from my village by Dogo."

"It is against the rule to give you too kinds of helps at a time. But I will help you now to become to your usual form.

"But I am quite sure that after you have become to your usual form, the Satyr will find you out and he shall

119

fight you probably to death if you don't struggle hard to fight him to death."

After the gnome explained to Simbi like that, he rubbed her body with his left palm and at the same time Simbi changed to her usual form, and all the pains of the beats went away. She was then in sound health and was so powerful that if she dashed to a tree it would fall down at once.

Then she knelt down and thanked the gnome greatly. After that he disappeared and then Simbi left that place at the same time so that the Satyr might not meet her in that there.

Having travelled for about one week, she discovered the hole in which she put her three gods and in which she was living before she was caught from the illusive hall and then transformed into the rock.

She entered the hole, she took the gods, she hung the satchel in which all were kept on her left shoulder. After that she left there and started to roam about.

After a while she travelled to a dam. She stopped there, she drank the water to her satisfaction, she bathed, after that she washed her gods as if they were human. Having done that, she sat at the bank of the dam, she waited until the sediment of the water went down, so that she could see her shadow clearly from the water. Then she lowered her head towards the water. And her shadow proved that the hairs of her head had scattered and very rough. Then she washed them again and having dried them, she parted them and wove all into six plaits. Having done that she cut about one fathom of rope which was a little thicker than the sewing thread. Then she stitched her cloth with the rope, because it had already torn in rags, after that she put it on. Then she looked at the water again. But her shadow proved that her beauty was disqualified by one thing and that was the powder of the cam-wood. Luckily when she looked thereabout there was the very tree from which she could obtain it. She went there, having looked at the bottom of the tree, she saw some of it (tree) which insects had torn into the powder. She took as much as she liked and then she came back to the dam. She mixed the powder with some water. After that she rubbed her body with it.

Then she looked at the water again, but her shadow proved that her face still needed something that which would make it looked more beautiful. And she went to a dried wood. She took a part of it which had already decayed. She brought it back to the bank. She ground it with stone and then she rubbed her face with the powder which came out of it. After that she looked at the water and her shadow proved that she was then become a complete beautiful lady. She turned her hands, feet, back, etc. to the water but her shadow proved that she was in excellency dress.

But when she raised up her head and was thinking in mind as if she wanted to remember something which had been escaped her mind, the Satyr who had been looking about for her since when she had left the rock, appeared to her at that moment.

"Hah! you are the noxious creature indeed and the death of this Dark Jungle, as the people are saying!"

Simbi wondered and frightened greatly immediately the Satyr appeared to her.

At the same time she ran to the spot in which her gods were drying in the sun. She put them back into the satchel and hung it on her left shoulder. Then she stood firmly on the bank of the dam.

She exclaimed without being feared of anything that the Satyr might do to her, "Come along, I am ready now to fight you to death! you hopeless evil creature, the death of the wayfarers! the cannibal of the Dark Jungle! Come on now, I am ready to fight with you!"

"Heh, I am sorry to tell you now that I have been thinking in mind before I met you here, that if I catch you I should keep you alive in the cage for a few days before I should kill you and eat your meat. But I am going to kill you now, because of your proud speaking!"

As the Satyr was still roaring on Simbi, more than one thousand of the evil creatures heard and came there. They surrounded the dam. All were shouting with joy for they put hope on the Satyr that no doubt he would kill Simbi within two seconds.

With pride, the Satyr jumped on to the bank of the dam. He slapped Simbi's head so heavily that she shrank to the size of one foot tall at the same moment. But as he was trying to take her away, she jumped up and immediately she fell down she became to her usual height. Without hesitation, she slapped his eyes and he became blind at the same time, but as Simbi was trying to push him into the dam and then to press his head down until he would die inside the water, he rubbed his eyes with palm and at the same moment, he gained his eyesight back. But when he breathed heavily on both his palms, both became as hot as a hot red iron at once. And when he was trying to grab Simbi with the hot palms so that she might be burnt to death, having seen this Simbi dived into the water. But the Satyr jumped into the water as well, he was searching for her just to grab her with the hot palms.

As he was still struggling to find her out from the bottom of the water, Simbi had changed into the water insect, she was swimming about on the surface of the water, and that was the last power she had.

When the Satyr saw this insect as the only living creature in that water, he held it and was suggesting "This insect is called 'Iromi'. This lady [Simbi] told me the other day that we fought together and conquered me, that she could change into 'Iro . . .' but she did not say on that day that she could change into 'Iromi' and this is 'Iromi'."

Then he threw it back into the water and it started to swim swiftly about on the surface of the water at the same time.

The Satyr was greatly confused about the name 'Iro. .' which Simbi had told him that she could change to. When she was about to mention the full name of the insect "Iromi" to the Satyr at the first time that they had fought together, Rali whispered to her on that day— "Hah, Simbi, don't you know that a lady must not leak out all she could do to her enemy as this Satyr?"

123

But Simbi stopped at the same time when she was just mentioned "Iro . . ." instead of "Iromi" immediately she heard the warning from Rali.

A few minutes later, the Satyr grabbed this insect again. He looked at it for about five minutes. "This is 'Iromi' and not 'Iro . . .' as the lady had mentioned into which she could change." Then he threw it back into the water and all of the rest evil creatures who surrounded the dam were looking at him as how he was suggesting within himself about the "Iromi" which Simbi had abbreviated to "Iro . . .".

Having thrown it back into the water, he did not go away but he was keeping watch of the time that Simbi would come out from the water.

After a while, the insect flew out of the water and entered into his nose unexpectedly. And at the same time it was biting his nostril so severely that within five minutes he was unable to bear the pain any longer. Then he was running about, he was crying loudly, he blew the air out from the nostril but the insect did not come out. He jumped up and down, he dashed to the trees and rocks but the insect was still biting him severely. As he was doing all these things the rest evil creatures were following him about and were laughing at him, with the intention that he was simply playing.

But when he fell down and died, they feared greatly and then they ran away.

When he was falling to the ground he shouted so horribly that everything became quiet at the same moment. His voice nearly rooted out all the big trees and the rocks and the mountains were nearly to blow up as well.

After he fell down and died, then the insect flew out of his nostril and then changed back to Simbi at once.

Thus Simbi killed the Satyr of the Dark Jungle, the noxious guard.

Then Simbi left there with gladness. She was wandering about in this Dark Jungle without being feared of any creature because she had killed the most harmful one, the Satyr.

One day, as she was going along as fast as she could, she came to the house of the Satyr which was behind of a rough hill. The surroundings of the house were so fearful that a person who was not brave could not go near there. But being Simbi had become a brave lady by that time, she entered the house.

When she travelled round it, she saw Rali in a cage at the back yard. She ran to the cage, she forced it open and then Rali came out. They embraced each other with gladness.

"Hah, I am glad as you come to safe me because there is no doubt, the Satyr shall kill me in a few days time, because he had told me about that before he went out since four days ago. Of course, he has not returned home since that day!" Rali explained with gladness.

"What about Kadara, Sala, Bako, the cockish lady, and the nameless refugees?" Simbi asked softly.

"The Satyr had killed and eaten all of them, but he ate Bako, the cockish lady, last," Rali replied.

"Is that so? It is sure then that they were destined to

125

be killed by the Satyr. Oh! which means, they have preceded the Satyr to heaven? Although, the Satyr himself is now in heaven and he is now dining with the inhabitants of heaven," Simbi said.

"Satyr is in heaven or what do you say now?" Rali wondered greatly.

"Yes, I have killed him about two days ago with the help of my three gods!" "Killed what?" Rali wondered.

"I say I have killed the Satyr, the owner of this house!"

"Did you fight with him before you could kill him?" Rali asked sharply.

"I changed into the water insect, 'Iromi' which I mentioned 'Iro . . .' when you told me the other day not to leak out all I could do. The Satyr was confused greatly about it, for he did not understand that it was 'Iromi' was shortened to 'Iro . . .'. And when I changed into it, I ate his nostril until he fell down and died, thus I killed him.

"Although he had changed both my feet and arms into the rock and I was saved by the gnome otherwise the Satyr and the rest evil creatures, would punish me to death," Simbi explained.

"What have happened to you after you have taken away by an eagle the other day?" Rali asked.

"Yes, I spent about one or two weeks inside the hole of the tree in which the eagle threw me. But I was saved out by a woodcutter who took me to his town. He married me and I had two issues. But I left him when my two sons were sacrificed to their king's gods so that they might be saved from the famine." "How did you manage to get the three gods?" Rali asked patiently.

"I got them from an old woman to whom I pawned myself so that I might get money to buy food and clothes, and I was taken away from her by the Satyr."

After Simbi had explained all she had experienced to Rali, they went round the Satyr's house again. Simbi took one of the Satyr's cudgels of bone, and after, they went out. They did not travel so far from the Satyr's house when they came to the fruit trees. They plucked as many as they could. They ate them to their satisfaction.

Having satisfied their hunger, they came back to the Satyr's house. When it was at night, they first attempted to sleep in that house. But when the house was too fearful for them, they took two leather bags which the Satyr had been using when he was alive. Each of the bags was big and long that it could contain two persons.

They came to the front of the house. Simbi entered inside one with her three gods and the cudgel of bone, after that she wrapped herself with it. Rali entered inside the second one as well and she wrapped herself with it, because the night was too cold.

When it was about one or two hours that both were enjoying the sleep, two tigers came there and thus they were coming every night to eat bones and rotten meat when the Satyr was alive.

When they discovered the two bags, they sniffed the smell and when the smell proved that persons were inside the bags, then they started to find the way just to go inside and then to eat what were there. But they did not see the way until they had twisted the bags to each other and then both seemed as one bag.

As they were trying to leave there having failed to get to the inside, their paws hooked some parts of the two bags. After they had struggled for some hours to take their paws away from them but were unable, then they were dragging them along in this Dark Jungle. Thus they were dragging them on and on and on until they had travelled near to the town of the multi-coloured people when it was about three o'clock in the morning. For the fear of the people, they struggled harder and the bags came out by accident from their paws and then they ran away for their lives.

It was like that Simbi and Rali came out from the Dark Jungle, of course the rest of them were perished there.

CHAPTER TWELVE

Simbi and Rali returned to their village safely

Simbi and Rali were still in danger. Because they must not appear in persons to the multi-coloured people and the people of the Sinners' town, otherwise the multi-coloured people would kill them as a revenge of the old woman's hen which Bako had stolen. And the people of the Sinners' town would kill them as a revenge of their king and chiefs that Simbi had been beheaded in the shrine the other day.

And they were going to travel on the Path of Death back to their village, because there was no another path from this Dark Jungle nearest to their village on which they could travel.

When the two tigers who brought the two bags near to the town of the multi-coloured people, left both there and then ran away for their lives, Simbi hesitated inside her own bag for a few minutes, she listened attentively just to make sure whether the two tigers were hid near there and then to eat them whenever they come out from the bags.

But when there was no sign which showed that the two

tigers were near there, then she came out from the bag in which she was. She told Rali to come out from the second one in which she was.

Then both sat near the two bags, they were thinking of how they could travel in the town of the multi-coloured people and in the Sinners' town without being suspected them as their victims.

After a while, Simbi remembered her gods which she hung on the left shoulder, and that time was about five o'clock in the morning.

She took them out of the satchel which was their home. She put them in a single line before her. After that, she asked from the god of famine the kind of a help that it could render so that the multi-coloured people might not be able to suspect them when they were travelling along in their town.

Having asked for such a help, within ten minutes, incalculable locusts rushed out from the heaven. They covered the town of the multi-coloured people so that it became so dark even more than the Dark Jungle.

Having seen this, Simbi packed the gods back into the satchel and at the same time they took the two big bags in which they slept before the two tigers dragged them to that place. Then they were travelling along in that town without being suspected them until they passed the town behind and then they started to travel on the Path of Death. The people of the town were unable to distinguish them from the natives because of the darkness that the locusts brought there.

A few days after, they travelled near to the Sinners'

town, they stopped and thought of what to do again so that the people of that town might not be able to suspect them. But Rali told Simbi to ask for a help from one of her gods. Without hesitation she asked from everyone of them (gods) but there was no reply, because time had passed long ago since she should had sacrificed a goat or ram to them, as the old woman who had given them to her had told her to be doing for them every time. But Simbi had neither goat nor ram to offer to them and they were hungry for the animal.

Having disappointed by the gods, she remembered to play a trick to any traveller who might travel to them at that moment. After a while, two men travelled to where they sat, but the two men were not the natives of the Sinners' town, they were wayfarers.

She stopped them, and they stopped at once because of her beauty which attracted them.

"Gentlemen, both of us have travelled until we are now unable to travel further. But with great respect I ask if both of you will be kind enough to carry both of us with these two bags, to the nearest of our village!" Simbi asked sharply with her attractive voice.

"We do agree to your request, but that will be when each of you have agreed to marry each of us!" The two men winked at each other that which showed they had lost all their senses in respect of the beauty of the two ladies.

"We do agree to marry you!" Simbi and Rali said loudly, but it was a lie.

After each of them had entered inside each of the two big bags, then each of the two men carried each bag.

Simbi and Rali returned to their village safely

But as they were carrying them along in the Sinners' town, a number of robbers saw the bags on their heads and they were following them just to steal the bags from them because they thought the contents were precious.

Thus the two men carried them away from the Sinners' town without suspecting them as their victims who had beheaded their King and some of the chiefs.

At last when the two men became tired they carried the bags to a town, in which they could get food to buy and to eat it, and then to rest as well till the morning— for it was in the night they came there.

Although this town was under the Sinners' town.

When they put the bags down, closely to themselves, those robbers came and sat with them. Sometimes they would be pressing the bags with hands just to make sure of the kind of the contents of the bags. And sometimes they would be joking with the two men. Of course, these two men did not understand all their tricks that they were just trying to persuade them to get chance and steal the bags from them.

Although, as the two men had almost tired before they came to that town, therefore immediately they had finished with food, which they bought, they fell asleep unnoticed. Then those robbers went away with the two bags, while Simbi and Rali were inside them. And they had carried both to their cave that which was in a very far jungle, before the dawn.

Having put them in their cave, they started to betray themselves, because everyone of them wanted himself alone to take them and for this reason they did not loose them.

Simbi and Rali returned to their village safely

After a while, when they were hungry and thirsty, their champion sent the rest for the two things. Having gone for the two things, he removed the bags to another far cave. And then he went out just to find the food and water, because he was quite sure then that the two bags were for him alone.

Immediately he left there, a man who had seen him with the bags when he was entering that cave, came and entered the cave. He took the bags away, for he thought as well that the bags contained precious things and he did not loose them.

As he was carrying them along, it was so he was looking here and there with fear of not being caught by the champion of the thieves, until he came to a high hill in the heart of a forest.

Having climbed it to the summit, luckily there was a very tall, mighty tree on the summit of the hill. Then he climbed the tree to the top, and he tied both bags onto one of the strong branches of that tree. After that he came down and went away with the intention to come back at night and then carry the bags to his town.

Having left, Simbi and Rali were struggling to come out from the bags but it was in vain, because the bags were very strong to cut.

But when it was about four hours that that man had left there, many monkeys climbed the tree to the top, just to eat its fruits. And as they were jumping from one branch and then to another they discovered the bags. But as the bags were very strange to them, because they had never seen or met such bags on tops of trees, then they started to cut a part of the bag in which Simbi was, with their teeth until she was visible to them.

As she was trying to come out through that space, they saw her and then they ran away with fear.

After she came out from her own, she loosened the second one in which Rali was and then she came out as well.

After that they plucked some of the fruits from that tree with the help of the cudgel of bone which she had taken with her from the Satyr's house. And then with great care of not being fall they went down from the tree and the hill.

Without hesitation, they started to travel along, and two days later they came to the Path of Death again. And when they travelled from the night till the day-break, they came to the end of the Path of Death and then they began to travel along on the path of their village.

When it remained one mile to reach their village, the first person that they met on the path was Dogo who had kidnapped and sold them long ago.

He had kidnapped three girls from their village and he was taking them to another town.

"Stop there, Dogo!" Simbi said loudly immediately she saw Dogo at a short distance from them. But he did not stop at all. When they came closely to each other, he looked at Simbi's face and Simbi asked sharply "Or don't you remember that you had been kidnapped me from my village long ago?" "Well, how many of you can I remember that I had kidnapped? I had kidnapped uncountable girls before you were born and uncountable when you were born and uncountable after I had kidnapped and sold you!" Dogo replied.

"All right, where are you taking these three girls to now?" Simbi asked impatiently.

"I am taking them to where I had taken you to, and they are going to travel on the Path of Death as you have done!" Dogo replied.

Then Simbi paused and she called onto her memory all the punishments and poverty, all of which she had experienced and she was very sorry for the three girls.

"You will not take them away on my presence, and I am going to revenge from you now all what you are doing to the girls of my village. It is this day you will stop to come there!"

But when Dogo wanted to take away the three girls, Simbi started to beat him with the cudgel of bone, and thus Dogo was beating her, but at last she overpowered him. She beat him until he fell down and then made a promise that he would not come to her village and would not kidnap anybody from there as from that day.

Having promised like that, Simbi, Rali and the three girls went to the village.

Nearly the whole people of the village followed Simbi to her mother's house. And her mother never believed her eyes when Simbi entered the house. But when she spoke to her then she believed that she was her daughter.

A few minutes after, those three girls whom Simbi took back from Dogo went to their houses, and Rali went to her mother's house as well.

Simbi and Rali returned to their village safely

The following day, Simbi's mother killed all kinds of domestic animals for the merriments which were performed in respect of Simbi's return, because her mother had lost hope that she would return.

Although she had nearly spent all her money for buying goats, sheep, fowls, etc. which she was sacrificing to all kinds of gods so that they might help her to call Simbi back home.

But within six months Simbi had become well known to all people in all villages and towns, in respect of the three gods which were given her by the old woman. The gods were helping all the people of her village etc. whenever they needed their helps.

Having rested for some days, she was going from house, to house she was warning all the children that it was a great mistake to a girl who did not obey her parents.

Having done that, she related the whole stories of her journey to her mother till the late hour in the night before she came to the end of it.

"Hah, my mother, I shall not disobey you again!" Simbi confessed to her mother when she remembered all the difficulties and the poverties which she had met.

"All right, my daughter, I believe, you will not disobey me again, and I thank gods who brought you back to me!" her mother replied sharply. "Good night, my mother," Simbi saluted her mother when she felt to sleep.

"Happy night rest, my daughter."

+